# JUST PLAIN NOT F

Stevie shrugged a
dramatic about th
just harmless fun.

"Sometimes son
mean or obnoxiou
on. "Or just plain

Stevie didn't spend a lot of time worrying about what other people thought of her. Usually she liked most people, and most people liked her back. Or so she had always thought. But now, for the first time, she began to wonder. Her jokes *were* funny. Weren't they? Or—the unwelcome thought floated into Stevie's mind, along with the angry faces of her brothers, Max, Veronica, and countless others who had been the victims of her wit—did her jokes actually annoy more people than they amused?

# THE SADDLE CLUB

# HORSE CAPADES

## BONNIE BRYANT

A SKYLARK BOOK

NEW YORK • TORONTO • LONDON • SYDNEY • AUCKLAND

RL 5, 009–012

HORSE CAPADES

A Bantam Skylark Book / March 1997

ISBN 0-553-48419-2

Published simultaneously in the United States and Canada.

Bantam Books are published by Bantam Books, a division of Bantam Doubleday Dell Publishing Group, Inc. Its trademark, consisting of the words "Bantam Books" and the portrayal of a rooster, is Registered in U.S. Patent and Trademark Office and in other countries. Marca Registrada. Bantam Books, 1540 Broadway, New York, New York 10036.

PRINTED IN THE UNITED STATES OF AMERICA

OPM      0 9 8 7 6 5 4 3 2 1

*I would like to express my special thanks
to Catherine Hapka for her help
in the writing of this book.*

"HERE SHE COMES," Stevie Lake whispered eagerly, poking her head over the half door of the stall where Carole Hanson was grooming her horse, Starlight.

Carole looked up. "Who?" she asked.

Stevie rolled her eyes. When Carole was busy fussing over Starlight—or any other horse, for that matter—she tended to forget about everything else. "Veronica, of course," Stevie said impatiently. "Her limo just pulled up. And my greatest practical joke ever is ready—just in time."

Now it was Carole's turn to roll her eyes. Stevie was one of her two best friends, and one of the things Carole and their other best friend, Lisa Atwood, loved about her was her wacky sense of humor. But sometimes even Stevie's best friends got a little tired of her practical jokes.

"Are you sure you want to pull something like this on Veronica right now?" Carole said, picking at a knot in Starlight's mane. "She's still pretty annoyed with you for putting her on that mailing list for Shoppers Anonymous. And if Max catches you, he might not be too cool about it considering that time last month when you put all the grain in the tool shed and all the tools in the grain shed." Max Regnery was the owner and manager of Pine Hollow Stables, where Stevie and her friends rode.

Stevie just grinned. "That was a good one, wasn't it?" she said. "A lot of work, but well worth it. And to answer your question, sure, I'm sure. There's no such thing as playing too many jokes on Veronica diAngelo."

Veronica was a spoiled, snobby rich girl who cared more about the color of her riding breeches than the condition of her horse. She owned a gorgeous Thoroughbred named Danny; he was perfectly trained and had a show record as long as her arm. But the thing that mattered most to Veronica was that Danny had been outrageously expensive.

"Normally I'd agree with you," Carole said, dropping her mane comb into Starlight's grooming bucket. "But just now I wonder if you ought to slow down before someone gets hurt. Like you, for instance." She was remembering all the times Stevie's practical jokes had gotten her—and sometimes her friends—in hot water.

Stevie just shrugged. "I know what I'm doing, okay?" she said. She sounded a little annoyed, so Carole decided not to say anything else. When Stevie was involved in one of her schemes, there was usually no stopping her.

At that moment a familiar voice floated down the aisle. "Oh, Re-e-ed!" Veronica called.

Red O'Malley was Pine Hollow's head stable hand, but Veronica treated him more like her own personal groom. Max believed that riding shouldn't begin when a person climbed into the saddle and end when they climbed out. He insisted that all the riders at Pine Hollow take care of the horses they rode, as well as help out with the stable chores. Stevie, Carole, and Lisa didn't mind Max's rules one bit. They loved horses so much that they wanted to learn absolutely everything about them. That was why the three girls had formed The Saddle Club. The group had only two rules: Members had to be horse-crazy, and they had to be willing to help one another with any problem, great or small.

Veronica, on the other hand, was never willing to help anyone with anything, unless it was herself. And that meant she ignored Max's rules whenever she thought she could get away with it. When her parents had first bought Danny for her, Veronica had spent a lot of time grooming him and looking after his every need. But once the novelty had worn off—in about an hour—she had returned to her usual habit of demanding that Red do most of the work for her. Lately she had grown even lazier than usual. Instead of arriving at Pine Hollow and then telling Red to get Danny ready for her, Veronica had actually started calling ahead so she wouldn't have to get to the stable any sooner than necessary.

Stevie grinned when she heard Veronica coming. "This is going to be great," she said. "I'm going to go get a front-row seat. Want to come?"

"Go ahead without me," Carole said. "I have some work to do here first, and I don't want to be late for the Horse Wise meeting." Horse Wise was Pine Hollow's branch of the United States Pony Club. Stevie, Carole, and Lisa were all members. At the moment, Veronica was a member, too, although she had been

4

kicked out more than once in the past for her unsportsmanlike behavior.

Stevie said good-bye to Carole and hurried down the aisle toward the locker room. On the way, she passed Lisa.

"Where are you going?" Lisa asked. She was busy fastening her shoulder-length light-brown hair into a ponytail. "It's almost time for Horse Wise to start."

"Belle's all ready," Stevie said hurriedly. "She's waiting in her stall. Come with me if you don't want to miss the fun."

Looking a little confused, Lisa followed her friend into the locker room. When the two girls arrived, Veronica had just pulled something out of her cubby and was staring at it with a mixture of surprise, annoyance, and disgust. She whirled around and immediately trained her eyes on Stevie.

"Stevie Lake!" she cried. "I know you're responsible for this stupid trick. What have you done with my gloves?" She held up a pair of fuzzy woolen mittens. They were hot pink with yellow stripes and bright green thumbs. Lisa bit her lip to keep from laughing.

Stevie gazed at Veronica with a wide-eyed, innocent expression. "You mean those aren't yours?" she asked. "But they're so elegant. So stylish. So . . . well . . . *you.*"

Veronica gritted her teeth. "Very funny," she said. "But I think it would be even funnier if I told Max about that history test we took last week, don't you? What was your grade again, Stevie?"

Stevie frowned. Max insisted that all his young riders maintain good grades at school. If a rider's average in any subject slipped below a C, that meant no riding until the grade came up again. Right now Stevie's history grade was dangerously near that line, and Veronica knew it. "Well, it wasn't my best effort," she admitted slowly.

Lisa glanced at her friend with a worried expression. She and Carole went to a different school from the one Stevie and Veronica attended, so she hadn't had any idea Stevie's grades were in trouble.

Veronica smiled in triumph. "I thought so," she said. "Now, I'm just going to ask you once more. Where are my riding gloves?"

"All right," Stevie said reluctantly. "Wait here." She disappeared for a moment. When she returned, she was carrying a pair of soft black leather gloves. "Here you go," she said, handing them over to Veronica. "I guess you win this time."

Veronica gave her a small, satisfied smile as she took the gloves and yanked them on. "I guess I do," she agreed. Then she whirled on her boot heel and left the room without another word.

Lisa turned to Stevie and raised one eyebrow. "That was it?" she asked. "That was the great prank you've been talking about all week?"

Stevie grinned, looking mysterious. "What do you think?"

Lisa sighed. She knew that expression, and it usually meant trouble. "I think we'd better go get our horses, or we'll be late for the meeting."

TEN MINUTES LATER Stevie, Lisa, and Carole rode into the outdoor ring. Most of the other students were there already, waiting for Max. Only Veronica was still missing.

But not for long. "Hurry up, Red," her voice came drifting out of the barn. "You're going to make me late."

Veronica emerged and bent down to tug at her boots. Lisa noticed that she was wobbling a little. She also noticed that the boots looked brand new.

"Looks like Miss Wardrobe didn't bother to break in her latest purchase before wearing," Carole said, as if reading Lisa's thoughts. Veronica was forever turning up at the stable in the latest—and most expensive—

riding togs. As in most things, the purchase price always meant more to her than anything else.

Lisa grinned. "It also looks like she might have gotten the wrong size," she said. "She doesn't look too comfortable." She turned to see if Stevie was enjoying the scene as much as she and Carole were.

But Stevie hardly seemed to have noticed. "Isn't she ever going to mount?" she muttered.

Lisa glanced at Carole and shrugged. Carole shrugged back. Sometimes their friend was hard to figure out.

"Come on," Veronica barked at Red, hobbling over to the mounting block near the ring. Ordinarily she didn't need the block to mount Danny, but The Saddle Club guessed that today her tight boots wouldn't allow her to mount any other way.

Red patiently led Danny to the block and held him while Veronica mounted. Once she was in the saddle, Veronica picked up the reins and rode away without a word of thanks. Red watched her go, looking irritated. But as Veronica turned Danny to ride toward the ring, the groom started to smile. Then he started to laugh. Veronica didn't notice, but Stevie did. She started to grin.

"What's going on?" Carole asked, looking confused.

A moment later, she knew. Veronica rode into the ring and the entire class got a good look at Danny. As the handsome Thoroughbred warmed up by trotting across the ring, there were titters, then chuckles, then guffaws from the other members of the class. Finally even Veronica started to notice that the other students were laughing at her.

"What?" she demanded, yanking Danny to a halt in the middle of the ring. "What are you all laughing at?" She narrowed her eyes suspiciously at Stevie, and her hand darted around to her own back. Stevie grinned, knowing that Veronica was remembering the time The Saddle Club had attached a POINT AND LAUGH sign to the back of her jacket.

When her hand came up empty, Veronica looked more suspicious than ever. She rode over to where Stevie was sitting on her horse, Belle, laughing helplessly.

"All right, that's enough, Stevie Lake," Veronica said crossly. "You'd better tell me what's going on right now, or I'll tell Max you're flunking history."

"Oh yeah?" Stevie shot back. "Then maybe I'll have to tell Max you called Red to tack up Danny for you—*again*." She knew that Max had given Veronica a stern talking-to about doing her own chores just last week. She also knew very well that Red hadn't been the one to tack up Danny today. Stevie knew that because she had volunteered for the job herself. "If you'd done your own work for a change and groomed Danny this morning, you would know what everybody's laughing at."

Veronica glared at her, then swung her right leg over Danny's back and slid down his left side, flinching a little when her tight boots hit the ground. Then she looked the horse over from stem to stern.

"I don't know what you're talking about," she said. "He looks fine."

At that, the watching crowd laughed harder than ever.

Doing her best to ignore them, Veronica walked around Danny's head and glanced at his other side. She spotted the problem almost immediately. Someone had written a message onto the right side of Danny's glossy dappled-gray hindquarters in what looked like red poster paint. It said SNOB ON BOARD.

At that moment Max came out of the stable and approached the ring. "Everybody ready to start?" he asked briskly.

He looked a little surprised when the entire class— minus one very angry member—just laughed in reply.

\* \* \*

10

"WASN'T THAT GREAT?" Stevie said for the fifteenth time. The Horse Wise meeting was over, and the Saddle Club girls were walking their horses around the stable yard to cool them down after a vigorous hour of jumping. "I thought that bright-red paint was a touch of genius, if I do say so myself. I even called Judy to find out what kind would be safe to use on Danny's skin." Judy Barker was the local equine vet.

"Great, Stevie," Lisa said, hoping she sounded more patient than she felt. Stevie had been gloating nonstop since the class had ended ten minutes earlier. Neither of the other girls had been able to get a word in edgewise—let alone change the topic of conversation to something more interesting.

"And did you see Veronica's face when she took off those fancy black gloves of hers and saw that her hands were red?" Stevie prompted.

Carole couldn't help grinning at that. "Don't you mean Luscious, Lustrous Red?" she said. That was the name of a shade of temporary hair dye. The Saddle Club had once used it to dye a skewbald horse to look like a chestnut. The hair dye had also worked quite well as a temporary hand dye inside Veronica's gloves. It had been the crowning touch on Stevie's practical joke.

"You're just lucky her gloves are black so the dye

11

didn't ruin them," Lisa said, pausing by the water trough to let her horse, a long-legged Thoroughbred mare named Prancer, take a few sips. "I doubt you could afford to replace them. She probably had them tailor-made in Paris or something."

"Lucky, my foot," Stevie replied. "It was all part of my plan. Why do you think I substituted the mittens for *those* gloves and not any of the four other pairs she had in her cubby?"

She looked so proud that Carole and Lisa gave in and laughed. Even though Stevie had been going a little crazy with the practical jokes lately, they had to admit that this one had been funny.

"It's too bad Max wasn't amused, though," Carole said as the three girls continued walking their horses around the yard.

"Don't be so sure," Stevie said. "I admit, he chewed me out pretty well after class. But I would swear there was a twinkle in his eye while he was doing it. I mean, he had to know why I was able to volunteer to tack up Danny, and why Veronica didn't notice. Only she would just mount on her horse's near side without even glancing at the rest of him. Oh, yes, I think Max might have been more amused than he let on."

"Maybe," Lisa said dubiously. "But didn't you say

the same thing after he yelled at you for the grain shed prank?"

"*And* after he scolded you for painting a smiley face on the tack room door?" Carole said.

Lisa nodded. "What about the time she dyed all the grain green for St. Patrick's Day? You thought he looked pretty amused then, too, but I for one didn't see it." She patted Prancer on the neck as the mare snuffled at her hair.

"Don't forget the time she hid in Delilah's stall and started telling Simon Atherton in a horsey voice to stop jabbing her in the ribs when he rode," Carole added. "He went screaming down the aisle and scared all the horses."

"That was pretty good, wasn't it?" Stevie mused. "I mean, I wouldn't have done it if I'd known he would react that way, but it *was* funny. And the horses all calmed down eventually." She smiled proudly. "I thought I was the master of practical jokes before. But I'm even better than I thought! Did I tell you about my moving image class project for school?"

It was an abrupt change of subject, even for Stevie. More importantly, it was a strange change of subject. Stevie rarely, if ever, talked about school.

"You mean the movie you were supposed to make?"

13

Lisa asked. She vaguely remembered Stevie complaining about the project a couple of weeks before. "What about it?"

Stevie was taking an elective class this term about film and television. The teacher's latest assignment was for each student to make a ten- to fifteen-minute film adaptation of a classic fairy tale. Students whose families didn't own camcorders were allowed to borrow the school's equipment. But the Lakes had bought a state-of-the-art video camera the Christmas before, and Stevie had already used it to complete several assignments for the class.

"I created a masterpiece," Stevie said. Belle snorted and nodded as if in agreement, and Stevie scratched her horse's neck fondly.

"What fairy tale did you do?" Carole asked. "And when did you do it? You've been at Pine Hollow with us practically every second for the past few weeks."

"I know," Stevie said. "That's the best part. The movie was a snap to make. All I did was set up the camera in Alex's bedroom and film him while he was asleep. I hid the camera behind the model planes on his dresser, and he never suspected a thing. It's great. I have fifteen minutes of him in his old Batman pajamas, grunting, drooling, and murmuring some girl's

14

name." Alex was Stevie's twin brother. Stevie also had a younger brother named Michael and an older brother named Chad.

Carole looked confused. "How are you planning to pass that off as a classic fairy tale?"

Stevie grinned. "That's easy. I'm calling it *Sleeping Beauty*."

Carole laughed, but Lisa looked worried. Of the three girls, she took school the most seriously, and she always worked hard on her assignments. "I don't know, Stevie," she said. "It's pretty funny, but do you think your teacher will like it? And don't you think Alex will be awfully mad when he finds out?"

"That's the point," Stevie said. "I'm killing two birds with one stone. This is the perfect way to pay Alex back for the time last month when he released Michael's entire cricket collection in my bedroom." She grimaced. "All that chirping kept me up every night for a week. But this will get him back. My teacher says she's going to show the best films to the entire school during weekly assembly. And I'm sure mine will be one of them. My teacher loves it when we're clever. This kind of thing is right up her alley."

Carole glanced at Starlight. She was ready for a change of subject, and her horse was ready for a good grooming and some fresh hay. "I think these guys are ready to go in," she said. "Shall we?"

"Sure," Lisa agreed. "I'll see you both in the tack room in a little while."

It only took the girls a few minutes to make their horses comfortable. Then they all met in the tack room to clean their saddles and bridles. It was one of their favorite locations for Saddle Club meetings. Max and his mother, Mrs. Reg, who helped run the stable, liked to see their riders keeping busy. But they didn't mind if they talked while they worked.

Lisa decided to head off the conversation before Stevie started talking about her pranks again. "Can you believe Max's announcement today? What a great surprise—I can't wait for the competition," she said. "It should be fun."

"Definitely," Carole said, picking up the saddle soap. She had been dying to discuss this subject with her friends ever since the end of class. But Stevie's rehashing of the Great Veronica Prank hadn't allowed it until now. "We don't have much time to prepare, though."

That day during the Horse Wise meeting, Max had made a surprise announcement. There was a brand-new Pony Club in the next town, and the members were eager to see an established club in action. Max

16

had invited them to Pine Hollow to see Horse Wise give a riding demonstration. Best of all, he had decided that a fun and interesting demonstration for the new club would be a small-scale hunter competition, complete with ribbons. It would take place in two weeks. There hadn't been any kind of show at Pine Hollow in quite a while, and all the riders were excited at the news.

"What are you going to put down as your goal?" Lisa asked Carole. Max always asked each of his young riders to write down a personal goal before each show they competed in. After the show, they were all supposed to think about whether they had met their goals, and why (or why not). Lisa had learned that there could be other goals besides winning a ribbon, and that a rider could learn a lot even if she didn't win anything.

"I'm not sure," Carole said thoughtfully, pausing to wipe a bit of soap off her chin. "I might put something about trying to keep Starlight focused before our round. He still reacts to an audience." Starlight was relatively young. When he heard applause, he sometimes became distracted and forgot what he was supposed to be doing. Carole was almost always able to remind him, but she knew it would be better if he wasn't distracted in the first place.

17

"That sounds good," Lisa said. "I think I'll make my goal trying to maintain an even pace through the course. That's so important in hunter events, and it just so happens that Prancer and I have been working on it a lot lately."

Carole nodded approvingly. "What about you, Stevie?"

"I don't know," Stevie said with a shrug. "I'm sure I'll think of something." The truth was, she had been so involved in her joke on Veronica that she had hardly paid attention to what Max was saying. But now that the news had had a chance to sink in, she was starting to get as excited as her friends. Stevie loved competing, and Belle was a good jumper. Lately Stevie had spent more time working with her on dressage, but there were two weeks before the competition—that would give Stevie and Belle plenty of time to work on their jumping form. In hunter competitions, horses and riders were expected to display smooth, even pacing and proper form, in addition to clearing all the fences. A horse that moved or jumped choppily was sure to finish out of the ribbons.

"Do you think Max will let us invite guests?" Stevie asked. "I bet Phil would love to come and see me win a blue ribbon." Phil Marsten was Stevie's boyfriend. They had met at riding camp. Phil lived in a town about ten miles away, so he and Stevie didn't see each other as much as they would have liked. But they attended one another's shows and Pony Club events as often as they could.

"I don't know," Carole said. "It wouldn't hurt to ask. But you might want to wait a few days to give Max a chance to forget about your latest little prank."

Just then the door opened and the subject of that prank walked in, carrying Danny's tack. Veronica frowned when she saw The Saddle Club. Her hands were still streaked with red dye.

"Oh, excuse me," Veronica spat. "I didn't realize there was a meeting of the Sad-*Dull* Club going on in here." Then, after dumping her dirty saddle and bridle, she whirled and stomped out, slamming the door behind her.

Stevie grinned. Being the master of practical jokes sure felt good.

STEVIE WASN'T FEELING so good about her pranks the following Monday afternoon. Her moving image teacher, Ms. Vogel, had asked Stevie to stay after school to talk about her version of *Sleeping Beauty*.

"But it was supposed to be clever," Stevie said helplessly, slumping down in her chair to avoid the stern look her teacher was giving her. It was already clear that Ms. Vogel's reaction to the film wasn't the one Stevie had been expecting. "*Sleeping Beauty.* Get it?"

Ms. Vogel leaned back against her desk and crossed her arms. "Stevie, I have to admit I'm disappointed in you. I would have thought you would know the difference between being clever and being lazy. Not to mention hurtful. I don't think your brother would appreciate having that film shown in front of the entire school at assembly, do you?"

"I guess not," Stevie muttered.

"That's why I'm asking you to redo the project," Ms. Vogel went on.

Stevie gulped. "Redo it?" she exclaimed. She had spent the last few minutes trying to prepare herself to take a low grade on her film. But she hadn't imagined the teacher would make her do it over. When would she have time, with the Pony Club competition coming up in less than two weeks? Stevie would have to put in a lot of hard work at the stable between now and the show if she expected to win a ribbon.

"Redo it," Ms. Vogel repeated firmly. "Your new film is due exactly two weeks from today. And it had better be good this time. I'd hate to see you fail this assignment."

*Not as much as I'd hate it*, Stevie thought grimly. At her teacher's last words, all thoughts of the hunter event flew out of her mind. She hadn't even considered the possibility that she might get a failing grade on her film. If that happened, it would mean no riding at all until she brought the grade up. Suddenly redoing her project didn't sound quite so bad.

"Don't worry, Ms. Vogel," Stevie said quickly. "I'll do better this time. I promise."

"I certainly hope so," the teacher said. "I think you have potential, Stevie. I really do. You have a truly creative mind. But you don't always use it in the best way. You like to make people laugh. But how often are those laughs at the expense of others? People like your brother?"

Stevie shrugged, not sure what she was supposed to say to that. She didn't know what Ms. Vogel was getting so worked up about. Alex and Stevie embarrassed each other all the time, and they both always survived. As far as Stevie was concerned, it was just one of the things that made life interesting.

"The truth is, Stevie, you have to be careful," the teacher went on, standing up and pacing back and forth in front of Stevie's desk. "Sometimes practical jokes can backfire. And sometimes your audience doesn't appreciate them as much as you think they will. That can make you unpopular pretty fast."

Stevie shrugged again. Ms. Vogel was being awfully dramatic about this whole thing. Stevie's jokes were just harmless fun. Nobody minded them—did they?

"Sometimes something you think is funny can seem

mean or obnoxious to someone else," Ms. Vogel went on. "Or just plain not funny."

Stevie didn't spend a lot of time worrying about what other people thought of her. Usually she liked most people, and most people liked her back. Or so she had always thought. But now, for the first time, she began to wonder. Her jokes *were* funny. Weren't they? Or—the unwelcome thought floated into Stevie's mind, along with the angry faces of her brothers, Max, Veronica, and countless others who had been the victims of her wit—did her jokes actually annoy more people than they amused?

Ms. Vogel wasn't finished. "Creativity should be about doing something bigger or better or more original, Stevie, not just finding a way to get away with something. Because if what you're doing is trying to get away with something, someday all your so-called creativity is going to catch up with you. And I'd hate to see that happen to you." The teacher stopped her pacing and perched on the edge of her desk again. She gave Stevie a long, searching look. "Does what I'm saying make any sense to you at all?"

"Yes," Stevie replied. And she meant it. She'd been trying to get away with things—especially her schoolwork—for too long. And now that she thought about it, the practical jokes really had been flying fast and furious lately. It *had* almost caught up with her—it had almost cost her her riding privileges. She had had a lot of close calls in the past, but this one was too close for comfort. She didn't intend to risk any more close calls anytime soon.

STEVIE WALKED TO Pine Hollow slowly, hardly noticing the light rain that was beginning to fall. She was still thinking about her conversation with her teacher. The day before, she had agreed to meet Carole and Lisa right after school to practice for the competition, and she was already late. But they could wait a few more minutes.

Normally Stevie didn't pay much attention to the lectures she was always getting from adults—teachers, parents, Max, and the rest. She wasn't sure why this one was different. It could be because Ms. Vogel had made her wonder, for the first time, how her constant practical jokes were really received by their victims and onlookers.

She thought about her latest masterpiece. The whole riding class had laughed at the sign on Danny's flank. But now that she thought about it, Stevie realized that Carole and Lisa had seemed less impressed with the whole thing than she herself had been. Now that she thought about it, she wasn't entirely sure that Max had been amused by it after all. She suspected he didn't like Veronica any more than anyone else, but another thing he didn't like was having his riding classes disrupted. In fact, he hated it. And she realized she was lucky he hadn't revoked her riding privileges on the spot.

The more Stevie thought about it, the more she realized she'd been riding on borrowed time for a while now. She could hardly count all the close calls she'd had because of her practical jokes. Max had threatened on more than one occasion to ban her from Pine Hollow. Usually she was pretty sure he was kidding, but still . . . Then there were all the times Stevie's teachers had kept her after school because of some harmless little joke, cutting into her valuable riding time. And once her parents had grounded her because of a prank she had pulled on one of her brothers. That time, Stevie hadn't been allowed anywhere near Pine Hollow—or Belle—for almost a week.

By the time she walked up Pine Hollow's long driveway, Stevie had reached an important decision. The rewards just weren't worth the risks anymore. She was through with practical jokes. Forever.

* * *

25

STEVIE FOUND HER friends practicing in the indoor ring to escape the rain, which was falling harder now, drumming steadily on the stable roof. She paused in the doorway and watched as Lisa took Prancer through a small course of fences. Prancer took each jump perfectly, tucking her hind feet up neatly behind her to avoid nicking any of the rails.

Stevie smiled, impressed. Her friend had worked hard with Prancer, a high-strung, spirited mare who had begun life as a racehorse. Prancer hadn't been jumping for long, and it was partly thanks to Lisa's dedication that she was doing so well at such a young age. When Lisa did something, she liked to do it right. That was one of the things Stevie admired most about her friend.

"There she is," Lisa called, spotting Stevie walking into the ring.

Carole turned and waved. "Sorry we didn't wait for you," she said. "Hurry up and get Belle ready. We're working on jump position."

"In a minute," Stevie called back. "I wanted to tell you guys something first. And ask you a favor."

Carole and Lisa dismounted and led their horses over to where Stevie was standing.

"What's up?" Carole asked.

26

Stevie took a deep breath. "Favor first, I guess," she said. "I wanted to ask if you would help me make a film for my moving image class."

"Another one?" Lisa asked. She patted Prancer soothingly when the mare stamped her feet restlessly, as if eager to get back to work.

"The same one," Stevie corrected. "Um, my teacher didn't like *Sleeping Beauty* very much. I have to do the project over. And I only have two weeks to do it."

Lisa glanced at Carole and grinned. "Well, I won't say I told you so, but I told you so."

But Carole was frowning. "You have two weeks to do another film? That won't leave you much time to get ready for the Pony Club competition."

"I know," Stevie said. "That's why I need your help. Especially since this film has got to be really good."

Lisa nodded. "Of course we'll help," she said. "What fairy tale are you going to do this time? *Sleeping Beauty* again?"

"Ugh. I don't think so," Stevie said with a shudder. "I'll have to come up with another one. I'll start thinking about it tonight."

"Good," Carole said. "Then let's get to work." She turned and prepared to remount Starlight.

"Wait," Stevie said quickly. "There's something else

I want to tell you." She paused until she was sure she had both her friends' full attention. This was important, and she didn't want them to miss it.

"What is it now, Stevie?" Lisa asked.

Stevie cleared her throat. "I've made a very important decision," she said solemnly. "You guys were right. My joking around has gotten out of hand lately. And it's got to stop. That's why I've decided I'm not going to play any more practical jokes ever again."

Carole and Lisa exchanged glances. Then they burst out laughing, startling Prancer and Starlight a little. The horses snorted and tossed their heads, which just made Carole and Lisa laugh even harder.

"E-even Prancer and Starlight don't believe you," Lisa choked out, hardly able to speak because she was laughing so hard.

Stevie frowned. This wasn't the reaction she had expected. "What's so funny?" she demanded.

"Good one, Stevie," Carole said through her giggles. "You almost had me believing you really had some important announcement to make."

"Me too," Lisa agreed with a grin. "But come on, how gullible do you think we are? As if you'd ever give up practical jokes!"

"But I mean it," Stevie protested. She couldn't believe her best friends were laughing at her resolution.

Couldn't they tell she was serious about it? "The thing with my film project convinced me. It's not worth it. So I'm giving up jokes—cold turkey."

"The film project, hmm?" Lisa said thoughtfully, still smiling. "I wonder about that, don't you, Carole?"

Carole nodded, her eyes twinkling. "You mean, does she really have to redo the project? Or is all this just part of some elaborate Stevie Lake scheme?"

Stevie felt a little hurt. "Fine. Believe me or don't believe me," she snapped. "I'm going to go get Belle ready."

"Okay," Carole said, not even seeming to notice how annoyed Stevie was. She turned to Lisa. "Come on, we'll keep practicing until she gets back. I'm sure Max will be paying attention to our jump positions in the competition. . . ."

Stevie hurried out of the ring, her friends' laughter still ringing in her ears. But once she calmed down, she decided they had a right to be a little suspicious. She fetched Belle's tack and hurried to her stall.

"I guess I've tried to trick them pretty often in the past, haven't I?" she said to the friendly mare, sliding the bit into her mouth and the bridle over her head. "Still, they're my best friends. You'd think they'd be able to tell when I'm being sincere."

She finished tacking up her horse, then led Belle

down the aisle. On the way, she passed Veronica, who was heading for Danny's stall. Veronica gave her a dirty look. Stevie guessed she was still angry about the pranks she had pulled during Saturday's Horse Wise meeting.

"Be careful," Stevie said sourly. "Your face might freeze that way."

Veronica tossed her head. "You think you're so funny, Stevie Lake," she said. "But we'll see how hard you're laughing when I win the blue ribbon at the hunter competition." With that, she continued on her way with a confident swagger.

Stevie watched her go with a little frown. Ever since Veronica had gotten Danny, her bragging about winning had really been something to worry about. Despite her poorer-than-average attitude, Veronica was a better-than-average rider. And Danny was a spectacularly well-trained horse. He never seemed to put a hoof wrong, whether his rider was paying atten- tion or not. There was nothing Stevie hated more than losing to Veronica. Nothing. But how could she expect Belle to beat Danny the wonder horse—espe- cially when Stevie would be spending all her valuable practice time making another film?

Finally, Stevie turned back to Belle with a sigh. "Come on, girl," she said, clucking to the horse to get her moving again. "We've got bigger problems than Veronica diAngelo today." She sighed again, realizing just how true that was. Stevie led the horse toward the spot near the entrance to the indoor ring where a battered horseshoe was nailed to the wall. It was Pine Hollow's official lucky horseshoe, and no rider who touched it before going out had ever been seriously hurt.

Reaching up, Stevie tapped the horseshoe with her fingers. "I think we're going to need all the luck we can get if we want to win anything at that competition," she told Belle. "And I could use some extra luck for my project, too."

She turned and began leading Belle toward the indoor ring. The wooden doors were propped open, and Stevie could hear Carole calling instructions to Lisa inside. Stevie and Belle were just outside the entrance when a sudden, shrill noise broke the peaceful quiet of the stable. It sounded like a fire alarm and a car horn all rolled into one. Echoing off the low stable roof, the sound was terrifying.

Stevie gasped, and Belle jumped two feet to one side, rolling her eyes until the whites showed. After a few seconds, the alarm stopped abruptly. Before Stevie's heartbeat could slow to its normal rate, Veronica stepped forward from the nearest row of stalls.

On her face was a sweet, apologetic smile, and in her hand was a black plastic gadget about the size of a small flashlight.

"I'm *sooo* sorry, Stevie," Veronica cooed insincerely. "My personal safety alarm just went off by accident. I hope it didn't startle you."

"Your what?" Stevie gasped. Beside her, Belle was still tossing her head nervously. But fortunately, the mare wasn't frightened as easily as some horses. Otherwise, she might have panicked at the sound and reared or raced off, hurting herself, Stevie, or someone else.

Veronica held up the gadget. "My personal safety alarm. It's the latest thing. I carry it with me in my purse or my pocket, and if someone tries to mug me or something, all I have to do is press this button. Like this, see?"

Her finger moved toward a small gray button, and Stevie tensed, expecting the piercing noise to begin again.

But Veronica's finger paused a hair's breadth from the button, and she smiled. "Just kidding," she said.

Stevie didn't think it was funny. What's more, she didn't think the alarm had gone off by accident the first time. "You idiot," she said, glaring. "You're just lucky Belle isn't more high-strung, or she might have trampled you." *Or me*, she thought. "And you're lucky I wasn't in the saddle yet." Stevie remembered the last time Veronica's thoughtless actions had startled Belle. That time, Veronica had scared Belle by taking a flash photograph of her, and Stevie had taken a spill, ending up with a bad concussion.

Just then Red O'Malley raced around the corner, his freckled face pale and anxious. "What on earth was that?" he asked. "I heard an alarm—"

Veronica gave Red the same explanation she'd given Stevie, but Red barely paused to listen.

"Go check the horses in the aisle behind you," he ordered Veronica in a no-nonsense voice. "Make sure they didn't panic and hurt themselves. I'll check this aisle." He glanced at Belle. "Stevie, you'd better get Belle away from here. She looks all right, but she needs some calming down."

Stevie nodded. As a grumpy-looking Veronica began to do as Red said, Stevie and Belle headed into the indoor ring. Stevie moved slowly, talking to the mare soothingly.

But when she entered the ring, she dropped the reins and raced forward as fast as she could, leaving Belle ground-tied near the entrance. She had just seen that Veronica's dangerous prank had affected a more high-strung horse than her own. It was Prancer. The mare was dancing nervously at the far end of the ring, her eyes rolling and her mouth flecked with foam.

Lying on the ground beside one of the jumps was the motionless form of Lisa Atwood.

"Lisa!" Stevie cried, racing toward her friend. Carole had dismounted and was struggling to control Starlight, who seemed on the verge of racing off to join Prancer in the corner.

Stevie dropped to her knees beside Lisa. "Lisa, can you hear me? Are you okay?" she asked frantically, looking for a sign of movement. She wanted to reach for her friend and try to make her sit up, but she knew that could be dangerous if Lisa was badly injured.

At the sound of Stevie's voice, Lisa's eyes fluttered open, and her arms moved. "S-Stevie?" she said. "Is that you? What happened?"

35

"You fell," Stevie said. "I guess Prancer threw you."

Lisa shook her head a little, then sat up. "I know that," she said, her voice sounding stronger already. She tested her arms, then her legs. All seemed fine. "I meant, what was that horrible noise?"

Stevie breathed a sigh of relief when she saw that Lisa seemed to be in one piece. "Who else?" she replied. "It was Veronica." Quickly she explained what had happened.

"That idiot," Carole said. She had finally gotten Starlight under control and had joined her friends just in time to hear Stevie's story. "She just doesn't think, does she? Who else would bring something like that into a stable at all! She must have known it would freak out the horses if it went off!"

Stevie nodded, giving Lisa her arm to help her clamber to her feet. "I know," she said. "The worst part is, I think she may have set it off on purpose, because she knew Belle and I were there."

"I can't believe even Veronica would pull such a stupid and dangerous stunt," Lisa said. Now that she was sure she was okay, she was worried about Prancer, who was still working herself into a lather on the far end of the ring.

"Believe it," Stevie said grimly. "Are you sure

you're all right, Lisa? You didn't hit your head, did you?"

"No. I landed smack on my rear end," Lisa said ruefully, rubbing her backside gingerly. "That thing went off just as we were approaching the fence and Prancer jerked off to the side and sent me flying. It knocked the wind out of me, that's all."

"You were lucky," Carole said. She looked angry. But then she glanced over at Prancer, and her expression changed to one of concern. "Wait here," she told her friends. "I'll see what I can do with Prancer."

As she walked slowly toward the nervous horse, Red O'Malley hurried into the indoor ring. "Everybody okay in here?" he asked anxiously.

Lisa nodded. "Just about," she said. "Prancer threw me, but I'm okay. I think she is, too, if Carole can calm her down before she hurts herself."

"I'd better give her a hand," Red said, heading after Carole.

Before long, the two of them had Prancer back under control. She was breathing hard and still seemed a little jumpy, but she had tired herself out quite a bit and Lisa didn't think she'd have any trouble controlling her now.

"I guess I'd better get back in that saddle, huh?" she

said, rubbing her backside again. Like all good riders, Lisa knew that it was important to ride again as soon as possible after a fall. That way, both horse and rider were reassured and things could get back to normal.

Red nodded. "And I guess I'd better go up to the house and tell Max what happened," he said. He rolled his eyes. "I ended up checking on all the horses myself, since Veronica managed to get sidetracked in her own horse's stall when she was supposed to be helping me. Luckily they all seem fine. But I have a feeling Max will want to have a few words with Veronica about this little incident anyway."

Carole nodded. She was sure the groom was right.

Red closed the doors behind him as he left. Lisa was glad about that—other than Stevie and Carole, she would rather not have an audience right now. She took a deep breath and remounted. She felt a little nervous, as she always did after a fall, and realized she was clutching the reins too tightly. She forced herself to relax, loosening her grip and reminding herself that she had to stay calm and in charge. She was the only one who could let Prancer know that everything was okay. Within a few minutes, she was able to stop reminding herself to relax and just do it. Prancer was still a little jumpier than usual, but she was obeying her rider as well as she always did. Apparently the accident hadn't done her any real harm, Lisa thought with relief.

"Why don't you try taking her through the course once," Carole suggested. "Just to make sure she hasn't been scared off jumping or something. You'd better do it at a slow trot, though—she looks pretty tired."

Lisa nodded. She touched her foot gently to Prancer's side behind the girth and the mare moved forward immediately. Lisa guided her around the ring at a smooth trot, then turned her toward the first fence, her heart in her mouth. If they could make it through this course, they could put the whole incident behind them. Prancer seemed a little nervous when she saw the obstacle ahead, but she was obeying Lisa's instructions just as well as she had on the flat.

Carole and Stevie watched, holding their breath as the mare came to within three strides of the fence, then two, then one.

At that moment there was a sudden loud clatter and crash as Veronica flung open the double wooden doors and hurried into the ring. At the same time, she shouted, "Red! Danny's okay, but he spilled his water bucket, and . . ."

Carole and Stevie didn't hear the rest. They were watching in horror as Prancer skidded to a stop in mid-takeoff, startled by Veronica's sudden loud entrance. The mare's forelegs smashed into the jump, which collapsed with a clatter of rails and posts. Lisa was flung forward onto Prancer's neck, and the reins were jarred loose from her grip. She managed to stay in the saddle, and as soon as she regained her balance, she began trying to calm her badly spooked horse. Prancer tossed her head and skittered to one side of the toppled jump.

Stevie bit her lip, wanting to yell advice to her friend but knowing that that would probably just upset the horse even more. She could tell Prancer was on the verge of panicking again.

Carole was thinking the same thing. She was also watching Prancer's forelegs carefully, looking for any sign of lameness or other injury. Fortunately the mare's legs seemed fine. And Lisa was doing a good job of calming her. Within a few minutes Prancer was still, though her sides were heaving and she continued to toss her head every few moments. Starlight and Belle had been facing the door when Veronica had entered, so they were only slightly startled by the incident. Carole and Stevie kept them facing away from Prancer so that they would be less likely to pick up on the mare's fright.

The Saddle Club had almost forgotten about Veronica, who had been the cause of all the trouble in the first place. Then she spoke from behind them.

"Oh," she said, in a bored, haughty voice. "I guess Red isn't in here." Before the astonished Saddle Club girls could say a word, Veronica had turned on her heel and left the ring.

"Can you believe her?" Stevie fumed, clenching her fists. She felt like running after Veronica and giving her a piece of her mind.

But Carole had other ideas. "Never mind," she said firmly. "We can deal with her later. Right now we've got to help Lisa with Prancer."

Stevie knew she was right. Carole helped Lisa walk Prancer for a few minutes to calm and cool her. They checked her legs carefully but could find no sign of injury. Once she was satisfied that the mare hadn't been physically hurt, Carole urged Lisa to try jumping again.

"Are you sure that's a good idea?" Lisa asked, as Stevie hurried to replace the rails on the jump Prancer had knocked over. "After two scares, isn't she a lot less likely to want to jump?"

"That's why it's so important for you to convince her to do it," Carole said. At least she hoped that was true. She admitted to herself that she'd never seen a horse in this particular situation before. But she could tell that Lisa was nervous enough already, so she didn't voice her own doubts. "Get up there and take her through the course once. Then we can put all the horses away and take a well-deserved rest."

"Right," Stevie replied, rejoining them. "But I'm sure you meant Max's version of resting: cleaning tack. Right?"

Even Lisa laughed a little at that. That made it easier for her to remount. She stayed on the flat for a good long time, making sure the mare was giving her full attention to her rider. Meanwhile Carole and Stevie started working with their own horses, staying on the other side of the ring to avoid distracting Prancer. Finally, when Lisa was convinced that she and the mare were communicating well, she turned her once more toward the jumps in the center of the ring. "Here we go," she called to her friends, who pulled up and turned to watch.

Lisa patted Prancer on the neck and signaled for a canter. She rode the mare in a wide circle before turning her toward the first obstacle, leaving plenty of room for their approach. As soon as Prancer realized where she was being asked to go, her canter became choppy, and she soon slowed to a prancing walk.

Lisa frowned. "Come on, girl," she said, signaling

firmly for a canter and keeping the mare moving toward the fence. When the mare realized her rider intended to keep her on course no matter what, she seemed to give in. But instead of maintaining an even pace as Lisa was asking her to do, Prancer sped up, her canter turning into what was almost a gallop. Lisa tried desperately to control her horse's stride, but Prancer wasn't paying attention anymore. Her courage gave out at the last minute, and she skidded to a stop inches in front of the jump, narrowly avoiding a repeat of her collision.

Lisa bit her lip and did her best to regain the mare's attention. She finally got her moving again, turning her toward the outside of the ring. Once they were away from the jumps, the mare settled down almost immediately.

"Let's try that again, okay?" she said to the horse. She urged Prancer back into the jump course, determined to take a firmer hand with her this time. But it didn't do any good. Once again Prancer refused to jump, this time skittering off to one side at the last minute.

Stevie and Carole rode over as Lisa turned the mare away from the course again. "That didn't go too well," Carole commented, looking concerned.

"I know," Lisa said ruefully, her brow knit in concentration. "She seems to be listening, but when we get close, she flips out and stops paying attention to me. Let me try taking her over a different fence."

"Good idea," Stevie agreed. She and Carole watched as Lisa rode Prancer toward a different obstacle. The same thing happened. Once the pair got close to the jump, the mare seemed to fall apart. This time, she got within a stride of the fence. She gathered her hindquarters as if getting ready to take off, then apparently changed her mind at the last second. She whirled around, her front hooves clipping the lower rail, and nearly unseated Lisa again before dancing to one side, tossing her head.

It took Lisa a little longer to get her under control this time. When she finally succeeded, she looked to her friends for help. "What should I do now?" she asked, her face white.

"Let's try one more thing," Carole suggested. "I'll take Starlight over a couple of the fences. Once Prancer sees that, maybe she won't be so nervous."

She mounted Starlight and rode him toward the first obstacle. The big bay gelding didn't hesitate. He trotted with even strides, taking off at just the right point and clearing the small fence easily. Carole jumped Starlight over two more fences before pulling him off the course and trotting over to join Lisa.

"Try her now," she said.

Lisa nodded grimly and gathered up the reins. Giving Prancer a quick pat on the neck, she aimed the mare at the first fence again.

But the same thing happened. Prancer got within a few strides of the fence and then shied away.

"Don't push her," Carole said gently as Lisa, her expression determined, got ready to try again. "She's made it perfectly clear she doesn't want to jump today. I think you might as well put her away and let her rest now. Maybe she'll have forgotten the whole incident by tomorrow."

Lisa didn't think that was very likely. But it also didn't seem likely that she would be able to get Prancer to jump that day. "All right," she said sadly. She patted the mare's sweaty neck and dismounted. "Let's hope a good night's sleep will do the trick."

As the girls slowly walked their horses around the ring to cool them down, Carole shook her head. "I still can't believe how much trouble Veronica manages to cause all by herself," she said angrily. "It's just like the time she took that flash picture and made Stevie fall off."

Lisa nodded. "It's also a little like my very first day at Pine Hollow," she said softly.

"That's right!" Carole said. "I'd almost forgotten."

45

On Lisa's first day at the stable, Veronica had carelessly let a door slam, just as she had today. The noise had startled the horse Lisa was riding and made him run wild.

"That time she spooked my horse into action," Lisa said. "Today she spooked my horse into *inaction*." She smiled a little as she thought about the irony. But her smile faded quickly as she thought about how much work was likely to be in front of her and Prancer. She knew that horses, despite their limited intellects, can form bad habits rather quickly, especially if they learn them in a stressful or frightening way. Despite what Carole had said, Lisa knew there wasn't much chance that Prancer would go back to jumping normally the next day.

"Well, Veronica is just lucky I gave up practical jokes," Stevie said. "Otherwise I'd be ready to play a big one to get back at her for this."

Carole rolled her eyes. If Stevie still wanted to pretend she'd given up pranks for good, she wasn't going to argue. "Well, if Max really thinks she set off that alarm thing on purpose, he'll probably kick her out of Horse Wise again," she said. "That would be the best revenge of all."

The others agreed wholeheartedly with that.

\* \* \*

AFTER DINNER THAT NIGHT, Stevie went up to her room. She knocked a pile of clean clothes and some magazines off her desk chair and sat down. It took only a few minutes of digging through the piles of books and papers on her desk to locate the book of fairy tales she'd taken out of the library a couple of weeks before. After a grimace when she realized the book was four days overdue, she flipped it open to the contents page.

"Let's see," she muttered to herself, scanning the names of the stories. The more she thought about Ms. Vogel's speech, the more she realized that her new film was going to have to be awfully good. That meant she couldn't do some boring fairy tale like *Sleeping Beauty* this time. She was going to have to come up with a really great tale to retell.

But all the tales in the book sounded boring to her. There was no way Ms. Vogel was going to be impressed by another dull rendition of *Hansel and Gretel* or *Cinderella.*

*Be clever,* Stevie told herself. *Maybe I should do* Beauty and the Beast, *starring Veronica diAngelo as the beast,* she thought, smiling a little at the thought. *I could cast myself as Beauty.*

Suddenly Stevie sat up straight in her chair. She had just given herself a great idea.

"That's it!" she exclaimed out loud. "I'll set my fairy tale on horseback!" As soon as she said it, she knew it was the perfect solution. The clever part wasn't picking an unusual story, it was doing a familiar story in an unusual way. Wasn't that what Ms. Vogel had said—bigger, better, or more original? And what could be more original than a fairy tale on horseback? For that matter, what could be bigger or better?

Since her treatment would be so original, Stevie decided she might as well choose the most familiar fairy tale of all, *Cinderella*. She would simply do it as it had never been done before. Stevie herself would play Cinderella, of course. Carole and Lisa could be the nasty stepsisters. And who better to act as Prince Charming than her very own Prince Charming, Phil Marsten?

"It's brilliant," Stevie whispered to herself. She scrabbled around on her desk for a pencil and a blank piece of paper and began making notes. Instead of a fairy godmother, her version would have a talking lucky horseshoe. Instead of a royal ball, the couple would fall in love at a dressage exhibition. Instead of cooking and scrubbing, poor Cinderella would have to spend her days mucking out stalls and cleaning tack.

Soon she had most of it figured out. The only thing that wasn't absolutely perfect was that she couldn't think of anyone to cast as the evil stepmother. She thought about asking Mrs. Reg to play the part, then decided the kindly woman wouldn't make a convincing villain. And she was pretty sure none of her brothers would agree to dress up as a woman, even for a starring role in her film. Finally, she decided she'd just have to do without. The pair of wicked stepsisters would be enough, and Stevie was sure Carole and Lisa would be up to the parts. After all, Lisa had acted in local plays before, and Carole had perfected an evil cackle when she had dressed up as a witch a few Halloweens ago.

Stevie grabbed another piece of paper and continued to write. There was so much to think about. She would have to type up a script for her actors and come up with the appropriate props and costumes. She would also have to figure out how to arrange the filming so that she could direct and act in the film at the same time. But she knew she could do it; after all, famous actors in Hollywood did that sort of thing all the time.

Her mind almost bubbling over with ideas, she dropped her pencil and hurried over to the phone on her bedside table. She just had to tell someone about her brainstorm. She tried Carole's line, then Lisa's. Both were busy, and Stevie guessed that they were talking to each other. She tried Phil's number. Phil himself answered after three rings.

"Hi, Stevie," he said, sounding pleased to hear from her. "How are you? Did Veronica try to get back at you today for that joke you played on her over the weekend?" The couple had talked on the phone Saturday night, and Stevie had told Phil all about her practical joke.

"Sort of," Stevie said, twirling the phone cord around one finger. "But I'll tell you about that in a minute. First, I have an important question to ask you."

"Shoot," Phil said.

"How would you like to be a movie star?" Stevie asked.

"Huh?" Phil sounded confused. "You mean when I grow up? I hadn't really—"

Stevie interrupted him impatiently. "No, not when you grow up. I mean right now. I have to make another film for my class, and I want you to be one of my stars. This time I'm going to do a horseback version of *Cinderella*."

"Another film?" Phil said. "I thought you just handed one in."

"I did," Stevie admitted. "But my teacher handed it right back to me. I have to redo it." She filled him in

50

on her conversation with Ms. Vogel. "But it was all for the best," Stevie finished. "She made me realize I was spending too much time on stupid practical jokes. So I decided that's it. No more pranks for me."

Phil laughed. "Yeah, right."

"No, I mean it," Stevie protested. First Carole and Lisa, now Phil. Why didn't any of her friends believe her?

"Okay, whatever," Phil said, still chuckling. "And now you want me to star in some wacky version of *Cinderella*? Let me guess—you want me to play the mean stepmother. You're going to make me wear a dress, and then sell the tape to my sisters."

Stevie frowned. "Of course not. I want you to play Prince Charming." *Even though you're not being very charming right now,* she added to herself. But she didn't say it. She needed Phil to agree to be in her film. Sometimes movie directors just had to be tactful, whether their actors deserved it or not.

"All right, all right," Phil said. "I'll play along. Prince Charming it is. When do we start shooting?"

"Well, I need a day or two to get the script ready and stuff like that," Stevie said, leaning back on her bed. "How about Wednesday after school?"

"I can't do it Wednesday," Phil said. "I have a riding lesson. But I'm free on Thursday."

51

"Good," Stevie said. "Thursday it is." They talked about other things for a while, including the upcoming Horse Wise competition and Lisa's fall that day. Finally Phil had to hang up.

"I'll see you on Thursday," he said.

"Uh-huh," Stevie replied. "I'm looking forward to it."

"Me too," Phil said with a laugh. "Whatever it is!"

Stevie sighed as she hung up and got ready to try Carole again. She really had given up practical jokes for good. Why didn't any of her friends believe her?

"Sister dear, let us depart," Carole read. "We don't want to be late for the dressage ball." She let out a snort. "A dressage ball? What in the world is that?"

Stevie frowned. It was Thursday afternoon, she had just passed out the script for *Cinderella*, and her cast was already being difficult. "It's obvious," she replied. "It's a ball where the dancers are on horseback, doing dressage."

"That doesn't make much sense," Lisa pointed out. "Why would anyone bother to do ballroom dancing on horseback?" She was perched on the fence of the outdoor ring. It was a beautiful springlike day, and the girls and Phil had decided to practice outside. Their

53

horses were tied up nearby. Max had agreed to let Phil ride one of the stable horses, Diablo, though he had looked skeptical when Stevie had told him the reason.

"Don't ask such silly questions," Stevie told Lisa, deciding that in this case the best defense was a strong offense. She had spent two days perfecting her script, and she wasn't interested in editorial comments from the actors. "Now hurry up and read through the whole thing. Then we'll start practicing. I thought we'd begin with the dressage ball scene, since that will be the hardest. I'll be right back—I have to get some props."

She disappeared inside. But instead of reading the script, Carole and Lisa went back to discussing the same topic they'd been discussing all week: Prancer.

"She still won't go near the jumps?" Carole asked Lisa. She leaned back against the wooden fence encircling the ring, letting the stapled pages of her script fall closed. She had had a dentist appointment the afternoon before, so she hadn't been around for Lisa's latest attempt to get Prancer to jump.

Lisa shook her head. "No way," she said. "She's perfectly fine as long as we stay on the flat. But any time she gets near a fence, her ears go back and she just plain refuses. I don't want to force her, but I'm not sure what to do to help her. Nothing I try seems to help."

Phil had heard all about the incident, and the girls had already filled him in on the problem Lisa was having with Prancer. He knew that Lisa had been working carefully and patiently to make the mare feel comfortable about jumping again. She had led her all around the jump course. She had left her tied to one of the obstacles for several minutes. She had even trotted her over a series of cavalletti on the ground. None of those things bothered Prancer one bit. But the minute Lisa tried to ride her to a fence, Prancer stopped cold.

"It's really a shame," Phil said, glancing over at Prancer. The pretty mare was nipping at a small patch of grass growing below the fence. "I can't believe Max let Veronica get away with something like that. Someone could have been badly hurt. Lisa almost was."

"I can't believe it, either," Carole said. "But Veronica keeps insisting the whole thing was just an accident. It's her word against Stevie's suspicions."

"And mine," Lisa added.

Carole nodded. "Mine too," she said. "And probably Max's. At least he told her never to bring that alarm thing to Pine Hollow again. I guess he can't punish her for something nobody can prove she did."

"Innocent until proven guilty," Phil said. He propped one elbow on the fence beside Lisa. "I guess that applies even to rats like her."

"I know," Lisa said sadly. "But it doesn't help me figure out what to do about Prancer."

Carole reached up and patted her friend comfortingly on the knee. "Don't worry, Lisa," she said. "You're a good rider, and Prancer is a smart horse. We'll figure out a way to help her get over her fear of jumping."

At that moment Stevie emerged from the stable carrying a large red rug and several other items. Seeing that her cast was talking instead of reading their scripts, she let out a cry of dismay. "What's the big idea?" she said, letting herself into the ring and dropping her pile of props on the hard-packed ground. "You're supposed to be reading!"

"Sorry, Stevie," Lisa said, feeling a little guilty. Even if this whole movie was part of some elaborate Stevie scheme, as she and Carole strongly suspected, she figured they should at least play along until they figured it out. Besides, she figured they were pretty safe today—Stevie didn't even have the camcorder with her. "But I have an idea. Why don't we do a read-through?"

"What's that?" Phil asked.

Lisa hopped down off the fence. "It's what we did at the first rehearsal the time I was in *Annie*," she explained. "The whole cast just sat around in chairs and read their parts in the script out loud. That way everyone got familiar with the whole play right away instead of just concentrating on their own parts." She sat down cross-legged on the ground, a safe distance from where the horses were tied.

"Sounds good to me," Carole said, plopping down beside her and turning to the first page of her script. "Let's get started."

As Phil sat down beside Carole, Stevie gazed at them with her hands on her hips. She wasn't sure whether to get angry or be grateful. She was annoyed that her friends weren't taking her production seriously and that they weren't obeying her instructions. After all, she was the director, as well as the scriptwriter. But she had to admit that Lisa's suggestion was a good one. And if it was the way professional theater people did things, all the better.

Finally she gave in and sat down, completing the circle on the ground. "Okay, good idea, Lisa," she said. Directors could afford to be gracious, she decided. "Let's do it." She opened to the first page and began:

" 'Oh, dear me, what shall I do? My terrible stepsisters have left me to clean out the stable all by myself. Oh, poor me—poor Cinderella . . .' "

AFTER THEY HAD READ through the entire script, Stevie decided to return to her original plan and practice the dressage ball scene. She spread the red rug on the ground near the gate and asked the actors to mount. Then she sent Carole and Lisa out of the ring and made Phil and Diablo stand in the center. The idea, as she explained, was that in this scene, the "dancers" would enter, march down the red carpet, and "curtsy" to the prince.

"These horses can't curtsy," Carole pointed out bluntly. "Maybe if we were riding circus horses—or Lipizzaners from the Spanish Riding School—we could do it, but I don't think you can turn Starlight and Prancer into haute école stars in the next two weeks."

"Of course not," Stevie said. "They're not really going to curtsy. I'm going to do it with special effects. Just like in the real movies." She reached into her pocket and pulled out a large, juicy carrot. "Watch this." She stood about five feet in front of Starlight and Prancer and raised a carrot above her head so they could see it.

Prancer took one look at the delicious-looking snack and stepped forward with an eager snort. Starlight, not wanting to be left behind, moved forward a couple of steps as well.

Stevie jumped back, keeping the carrot out of the horses' reach. "Hey, you guys, you have to keep them under control," she told her friends. "Don't let them move forward."

Carole and Lisa shared a glance. Then, without a word, they signaled for their horses to step backward onto the end of the red carpet. Starlight obeyed immediately. Prancer, who was less experienced with this particular command, hesitated for a moment, then did as Lisa asked.

"Okay," Stevie said, when they were back in position. "Let's try this again." She held the carrot above her head.

This time, Carole and Lisa firmly ordered their horses to stay put, despite the tempting carrot. The horses obeyed. But when Stevie suddenly dropped the hand holding the carrot, the horses' heads followed. To an observer, the horses seemed to be bobbing their heads, almost as if they were—well—curtsying.

Stevie laughed out loud. She had been pretty sure the trick would work, but not entirely sure. Now she knew it would look perfect on camera.

"That was great!" she called. "Let's try it one more time, then I'll let them have their carrots as a reward."

She raised her hand over her head again, but this time, before she could lower it, she felt a tug on the carrot. She looked up, startled, and saw Diablo's big teeth nibbling at the top of the carrot. As the horse plucked it out of her fingers, Stevie whirled around to see Phil's grinning face.

"I guess the prince's horse didn't like the curtsies," Phil said.

Stevie stuck out her tongue at him in reply. Behind her, she could hear the wicked stepsisters laughing hysterically. With a sigh, Stevie pulled two more carrots out of her pocket and walked over to give them to the curtsiers. She was learning that it wasn't easy being a director—not to mention a special effects specialist.

"LEFT! LEFT!" STEVIE called frantically. Lisa heard her and quickly adjusted Prancer's stride so the mare was moving to the left. Unfortunately, Phil heard her, too, and thought the direction was intended for him. He turned Diablo to the left, too, almost running him into Prancer.

"Oops," Carole said with a giggle. She was sitting

astride Starlight nearby, watching the other two practice what Stevie called their ballroom dressage.

"Cut!" Stevie yelled, even though there was no camera in sight. She let out a noisy sigh of frustration. The dressage ball scene wasn't going very well. She had carefully worked out the choreography the night before, and she knew it would look perfect when the actors got it right. Or, rather, *if* they got it right. Right now it wasn't looking good.

"Sorry, Stevie," Phil said. "It wasn't Lisa's fault. It was mine."

"At least Prancer is obeying me whenever I ask her to do something," Lisa said, trying to look on the bright side. "Maybe that means she'll be ready to jump the next time I ask her to do that."

"Maybe," Carole agreed hopefully.

Stevie just grumbled under her breath. Normally she would have agreed that it was a good sign. But right now she wasn't feeling particularly concerned about Prancer's jumping. The only thing she was feeling concerned about was her movie. They had been rehearsing for almost two hours, and aside from the "curtsying" scene, nothing had gone right. On many past occasions, Stevie had seen her friends follow difficult jump courses and complete complex dressage tests without missing a beat. But today they couldn't seem to follow the simplest directions. And the horses were getting tired. They would have to stop soon.

"Should we try it again?" Phil asked contritely, noticing the thunderous look on Stevie's face.

She nodded curtly. "Take it from the top," she said. "Remember, Lisa, you move left while Phil moves right. Then you both start turning clockwise. One, two, three—go!"

Lisa urged Prancer into motion. The tall mare moved to the left. Diablo followed Phil's instructions, moving evenly to the right. Then Diablo swung into a clockwise movement—just in time to narrowly avoid another collision with Prancer, who was moving counterclockwise.

"Oops," said Lisa, pulling her horse to a stop.

Stevie just sighed. It was tough being director, scriptwriter, and special effects specialist, all right. But being a choreographer was no picnic, either.


"WHAT TIME CAN you be here on Saturday?" Stevie asked Phil.

Phil did a quick calculation in his head, then gave her a time.

"Good," Stevie said. "That means we can start rehearsing right after Horse Wise."

Carole and Lisa let out mock groans of protest, but Stevie just ignored them. After the disastrous rehearsal they'd just had, she was in no mood for kidding around. The worst part was that nobody else seemed aware of how much work they still had to do before *Cinderella* would be ready for filming. And Stevie's friends didn't seem to appreciate that her moving image grade—and, by extension, her whole riding career at Pine Hollow—was in jeopardy.

"Come on, let's go in," was all Stevie said. She led Belle out of the ring and toward the stable entrance.

At that moment, Veronica appeared in the doorway, leading Danny. She frowned when she spotted The Saddle Club. "I'm going to ride in the ring now," she said imperiously. "I hope you're finished fooling around out here. I have serious work to do—I have to make sure Danny's ready to win next Saturday." She gave a thin little smile. "Although there's really no doubt he can beat anybody at *this* stable, hands down."

Lisa scowled at her. Veronica's bragging was always annoying, but today it bothered her more than ever. Veronica didn't seem to care that she'd probably ruined Lisa and Prancer's chances of doing well in the competition—or even that Prancer might decide she never wanted to jump again. Her prank might have been intended for Stevie, and that was bad enough, but the fact that it had gotten Lisa instead and Veronica wasn't sorry made it seem even worse somehow. It was just one more example of the snobby girl's selfishness.

"Don't worry, girl," she whispered to Prancer as Veronica and Danny swept past them. "We'll show her. We'll have you jumping again before the competition—just you wait and see!"

5

"I'M SURE HE'LL be here soon," Stevie said, glancing at her watch. "Maybe we should go ahead and start without him."

It was Saturday. The unmounted Horse Wise meeting had ended a few minutes earlier, and The Saddle Club had just finished tacking up their horses for another movie rehearsal. They were waiting for Phil to arrive so they could get started. Stevie had left the camcorder at home again. She had the funniest feeling they weren't quite ready for filming yet.

"I have a better idea," Lisa said. "How about if you guys help me work with Prancer a little until Phil gets here? She's really been agreeable for the past couple of days about everything but jumping. Maybe today I can get her over some fences."

"Sounds good to me," Carole said.

Part of Stevie understood why Lisa and Carole were so eager to work with Prancer every chance they got. Normally she would consider this sort of problem a Saddle Club project and throw herself into it wholeheartedly. But she couldn't help thinking that her film should be a Saddle Club project, too. And Carole and Lisa weren't exactly going out of their way to help with that, were they? That was why the other part of Stevie was simply annoyed at the delay in her moviemaking.

"You two go ahead," she said, sounding grumpier than she had meant to. "I've got some things to get ready." She turned and headed back inside after tying Belle to the rail.

Carole and Lisa were a little surprised at Stevie's attitude, but they quickly forgot about it. There was no time to lose if they were to have any chance of getting Prancer into shape by next weekend's competition. If Stevie was upset about something, she'd tell them about it sooner or later.

Veronica had been practicing in the outdoor ring the previous evening, and she hadn't bothered to remove the small jump course she'd set up. For once Carole and Lisa were grateful for the other girl's laziness.

"I think we should take the top rail off a couple of these," Carole suggested. "We don't want to make Prancer try anything too high."

Lisa gazed at the jumps. They were higher than anything she and Prancer would try to jump even under favorable conditions. "I guess Veronica is pretty confident about Danny's jumping if she had him practicing over these," she said.

"She should be," Carole said as the two girls clipped their horses' lead lines to the gate and headed for the first obstacle. "Danny could handle these jumps and more without turning a hair. But that doesn't necessarily mean they'll win next weekend. Hunter competitions aren't just about getting over the jumps, remember? The rider has to do her part, too."

"I know," Lisa said. "But they're judging the horse. And right now Prancer won't even jump."

"That's no way to think," Carole chided as she lifted the highest rail off the jump. She carried it to the side of the ring and pushed it under the fence. "You know you have to try to keep a positive attitude. If you're worried, Prancer will sense that and it will make her worried, too. And that can only have a bad effect on her performance."

"All right, all right," Lisa said, laughing as she dragged another rail toward the fence. "Thanks, Teach. I'll try to stay optimistic. Now come on, we'd better hurry if we want to get any practicing in. Phil will be here any minute."

A few minutes later the course was ready. Carole and Lisa mounted and warmed up their horses by trotting them around the ring. Soon they were ready to start jumping. Carole took Starlight through the course first. The gelding trotted smoothly, clearing each obstacle with plenty of room to spare.

"There, we've shown you guys how easy it can be," Carole said to Lisa, pulling up her horse and giving him a fond pat. "Now you try it."

"Okay," Lisa said, taking a deep breath. "Here goes nothing."

Carole saw the look of determination on her friend's face as she sent Prancer toward the first jump. The mare pricked her ears forward as they approached it, then laid them back in consternation. She began shaking her head when they were only a few yards away, and did her best to stop short just in front of it. But Lisa urged her on firmly, using her legs, seat, and hands, as well as her voice.

"Come on, Prancer," she told the mare sternly. "Enough's enough. You can do this; I know you can."

Carole held her breath as she watched. Lisa wasn't giving in this time; she was giving the mare an unmistakable order. Would Prancer obey?

Finally, Prancer's years of training won out over her nervousness, if only by the narrowest of margins. The mare hopped forward, taking the tiny fence from a halt and barely clearing it. When she landed safely on the other side, she looked surprised. So did Lisa. But she didn't waste the momentum. Immediately, she urged Prancer forward once again toward the next fence. This time the mare didn't come to a full stop, though she slowed down quite a bit and jumped jerkily and sloppily. The third fence went much the same way.

Lisa pulled Prancer to a halt after that, looking pleased. "She did it!" she called to Carole.

Carole grinned back. "So I saw," she replied. "Nice riding!"

"Thanks," Lisa said. But her smile faded a little when she thought about the competition. It was only one short week away. Prancer had jumped, but hardly in ribbon-winning form. Lisa knew that winning awards wasn't the most important thing about riding—not even close. But she liked to do things the best way she could, and she hated to think that she and Prancer would lose their chance to do their best because of Veronica's mean trick.

She said as much to Carole. Carole looked thoughtful. "I know how you feel," she said slowly. "But you know what Max would say. You shouldn't be competing against the other riders. You should be trying to meet your own goal."

"I know," Lisa said. "But at this rate I can forget about the goal I wrote down. It was to keep an even pace through the course, remember?"

Before Carole could reply, she heard the sound of a car coming up the stable driveway. "That looks like Phil," she said, glancing back over her shoulder. "I guess that's the end of our jumping practice for now."

Sure enough, Stevie appeared in the stable doorway seconds later. "Finally!" she cried. She put her hands on her hips and tapped her foot impatiently as Phil climbed out of the car and said good-bye to his older sister, who was driving.

"Sorry I'm late," he called, jogging over to the ring. "Barbara offered to drop me off on her way to the mall, but she took forever getting ready."

"That's okay," Lisa said, smiling. "You gave us just enough time to convince Prancer to try a little jumping, for a change."

"Really?" Phil said, looking interested. "You got her to jump today?"

Lisa and Carole began telling him about it.

"Ahem!" Stevie interrupted loudly. "If you don't mind, we have work to do. You can talk about Prancer later."

Her friends looked surprised, but they stopped talking.

"Okay, director," Phil said. "What do we do first?"

Stevie nodded in satisfaction. That was more like it. Maybe this rehearsal wouldn't be a total loss after all. "First, go get Diablo. He's in his stall—I tacked him up for you."

Phil hurried off, and Stevie turned to Carole and Lisa. "You two will need to practice that curtsying scene some more, but we can do that later. First, I want to practice with some of the props I've been making."

"Props?" Carole said, glancing at Lisa with a smile. "Wow, you're really going all out with this one, Stevie."

"Of course I am," Stevie said. "I told you I have to get a good grade, remember?" But suddenly she realized what Carole really meant. She obviously still thought this movie was just a setup for some elaborate practical joke. Stevie frowned but decided to let it

71

pass. Her friends would surely realize she was serious when they saw the props. She had spent hours the previous night working on them.

Stevie walked over to her backpack, which was leaning against the stable wall. Reaching inside, she pulled out the first item and held it up. It was a U-shaped piece of blue cardboard covered in plastic wrap.

"What in the world is that?" Lisa asked.

"Isn't it obvious?" Stevie said in surprise. "It's the glass horseshoe."

Carole and Lisa laughed. "And you said you'd given up joking around!" Carole said.

"No, I said I've given up practical jokes," Stevie corrected her. "That doesn't mean I can't still have a sense of humor. Besides, what else would you expect in a horseback *Cinderella?*"

"Not a thing," Lisa said. "It's perfect. Now what do we do with it?"

As soon as Phil returned with Diablo, Stevie had them practice with the horseshoe for a while. All the two stepsisters had to do was dismount, signal for their horses to raise one foreleg, and then let Phil pretend to try the shoe on each horse for size.

"But Belle's feet are almost the exact same size as

the other horses',"  Lisa pointed out sensibly. "How are you going to show which horse the shoe fits?"

"Simple," Stevie said. She hurried over to the backpack again and pulled out another "glass" horseshoe. This one was larger than the other. "It's the magic of the movies. When it's Belle's turn to try on the shoe, I'll switch the too-small shoe with this one, which I traced around Belle's foot." She asked Belle to lift her leg, and demonstrated. "See? Perfect fit."

Phil laughed. "That's great, Stevie," he said with admiration. "Really clever."

"Thanks," Stevie said, smiling back at him. She was really starting to feel better about this rehearsal. Finally, everything was falling into place. And now that Prancer had started jumping again, maybe Carole and Lisa would be able to concentrate better.

But as the rehearsal continued, Stevie felt her optimistic mood slipping away. After practicing a little more with the fake horseshoes, Stevie had pulled out her next prop—a frilly pink parasol, left over from a couple of Halloweens before, when Mrs. Lake had gone to a costume party as Scarlett O'Hara.

"What's that for?" Lisa asked suspiciously as soon as she saw it. "You don't expect me to carry that hideous thing, do you?"

"Well, there's only one," Stevie said, "so only one of you can carry it." She reached into the bag again and held up a large Spanish-style fan, decorated with butterflies and flowers. "The other one gets to carry this."

Carole was shaking her head. "No way," she said. "I agreed to be in your movie. I didn't agree to look like an idiot on film."

"What do you mean?" Stevie asked. "These are just your props for the ball scene. You have to look like you're dressed up, you know. And we need to start practicing with them now so the horses won't be spooked when it's time to start filming."

"Are you kidding?" Lisa said. "I'm already spooked by them."

Stevie turned to Phil in exasperation, hoping he could help her explain to her friends how important it was for them to look the part. But Phil was glancing at his watch. He didn't even seem to be paying attention.

"Are we keeping you?" Stevie asked him sarcastically.

Phil looked up quickly. "What? Oh, um, no," he said. "Sorry. What were we talking about?"

Stevie explained the problem. But as she talked, she noticed that Phil kept shooting looks at the stable.

"Do you have to use the bathroom or something?" she finally snapped at him.

Phil blushed a little. "No, no," he said. "I'm listening. Really."

Stevie turned back to Carole and Lisa. "Come on, guys," she said. "I don't even have the camcorder here today. Can't you just try riding with the props—please?"

"Well," Carole said slowly, "since you asked so nicely, I guess we could try it. Since we're not filming today, I don't know what harm it can do."

"Thanks," Stevie said, relieved. "Lisa? What about you?"

Lisa shrugged. "All right," she agreed. "But if all the cute guys from my school suddenly show up to watch, you're dead meat. Oh, and I call the fan."

Carole stuck out her tongue. "Fine. I prefer the parasol anyway."

Carole, Lisa, and Phil laughed, but Stevie sighed. Directing a movie was turning out to be like pulling teeth—especially when she had to be director, scriptwriter, special effects specialist, choreographer, *and* props person all rolled into one.

Carole and Lisa were cantering around the ring with their new props a few minutes later when Red

O'Malley came out of the stable. He waved and called to Stevie.

"Cut!" she yelled to her actors. "Take five." Then she turned Belle and trotted over to see what Red wanted.

"There's a phone call for you, Stevie," Red explained. "I told the guy you were busy, but he said it was important."

"He?" Stevie said with a frown. "Who is it?"

Red shrugged. "He says his name's Starr. He's calling long distance."

"Okay, I'll be right there," Stevie said, puzzled. Could it be her brothers playing a practical joke? She didn't think so. She knew Chad had soccer practice that day, and Alex and Michael were fishing with their father.

She dismounted and handed the reins to Carole. "Hold Belle for a second, okay? I'll be right back." She followed Red inside and down the hall to Mrs. Reg's office. The woman was nowhere to be seen, but the receiver of her phone was off the hook.

"There you go," Red said. "See you later." He hurried away as Stevie picked up the phone.

"Hello?" she said tentatively.

"Is this Miss Lake?" asked a deep male voice. "Miss Stephanie Lake?"

"Yes, this is Stevie Lake," she replied.

"My name's Starr. Rex Starr," the other voice went on. "I'm calling from Hollywood. That's the movie capital of the world you know, young lady."

"I know," Stevie said. There was something slightly familiar about the voice, but she couldn't quite place it. "What do you want? Is this a joke or something?"

"No joke, young lady," Rex Starr said. "No joke at all. I'm calling to make your dreams come true. You see, I represent several major movie studios. And the buzz out here in Hollywood right now is that you're the hottest young director in the East. We want to buy the rights to your latest project, *Sleeping Beauty*. We hear it's a masterpiece. Absolute box office gold."

Suddenly Stevie figured out who the voice belonged to. "A.J.!" she shrieked. "Is that you?" A.J. was Phil's best friend and an out-of-town member of The Saddle Club.

"No, I told you, this is R-Rex S-S-S-Starr," the voice said, then collapsed into very familiar-sounding laughter.

It was soon echoed by laughter from behind her. She whirled around and saw that Phil was doubled over in the doorway. Lisa and Carole were grinning behind him.

"Gotcha!" Phil cried, before bursting out laughing once again.

Stevie wasn't sure how to react. Normally she would have thought Phil's prank was funny, even if she was the victim of it. But today the last thing she wanted to waste time on was practical jokes. Finally she slammed down the receiver and crossed her arms over her chest.

"Very funny," she said grumpily. "Now can we get back to the rehearsal, please?" She brushed past her friends and stomped back out to the ring, where Red was watching the horses.

Carole, Lisa, and Phil gave each other surprised looks. Was Stevie angry because they had pulled their practical joke before her own was ready—whatever it was? That wasn't like her.

"She can dish it out, but she can't take it," Phil muttered, staring after Stevie.

Carole just shrugged and sighed. "Come on," she said, heading in the direction Stevie had just gone. "We'd better get back out there."

6

"No! Bow, I said! Bow!" Stevie cried.

Carole looked over her shoulder. "Put down that camera, and maybe I'll think about it," she said. "I feel stupid enough doing this stuff with people walking by and looking at us every five minutes."

It was Sunday afternoon. Stevie, Carole, and Lisa were in the back paddock rehearsing *Cinderella*. Or at least Stevie was trying to rehearse. Once again, Carole and Lisa seemed much more interested in talking about Prancer and goofing around than they were in practicing their parts. Worst of all, Phil hadn't been able to make it at all.

They were rehearsing the final scene of the movie.

That was the wedding scene, where Cinderella and Prince Charming rode off into the sunset together while the jealous stepsisters are forced to bow to the royal couple. Stevie had decided that she would be lucky if she could get the horses to do the curtsying in the ball scene. In this one she had decided the stepsisters should dismount and do their own bowing. She figured that if they really got into it and touched their foreheads to the ground, it would still look pretty impressive.

The trouble was, they were very reluctant to do it right then. As always on weekends, Pine Hollow was busy. Despite the fact that they were rehearsing in the little out-of-the-way paddock behind the stable, plenty of people had already stopped by to watch what the girls were doing. Even when there was no audience, Carole and Lisa were reluctant to perform any potentially embarrassing moves—such as bowing and scraping to an imaginary prince—while Stevie was holding the camcorder.

"For the last time, I'm not filming this so I can play it at your next birthday party. And I'm not planning to set up a screening at your next school dance. And there's no way I'm going to send the tape into one of those video bloopers shows on TV. I swear. Cross my heart and hope to die. Okay?" Stevie said.

Lisa looked at Carole. "She crossed her heart. I guess she means it."

Carole nodded, then grinned. "So we haven't figured out what she's really up to yet. But we will!"

Stevie sighed. Her friends still didn't believe her assignment was for real. That meant they weren't doing their best to help her, as they would for a real Saddle Club project.

"Never mind," Stevie said. "That's enough bowing for now. Let's put the horses away. Then you guys can try on your costumes."

"Costumes?" Carole said. "I'm not sure I like the sound of that."

"What do you mean?" Stevie demanded. "You can't make a movie without costumes, right? They're great—you'll see. I stayed up half the night getting them just right."

After the girls had untacked the horses and made them comfortable in their stalls, they met again in the back paddock. This time Stevie was carrying a large duffel bag. She dropped it on the ground and began digging through the contents.

"Let's see . . . I had to get a little creative with these, since there wasn't much time," Stevie said. "But I found some good stuff up in the attic. I think it'll do." She pulled out a neon green T-shirt with the

81

words *I'm with Stupid* printed on the front. "Lisa, you're going to wear this for the opening scenes."

"Like heck I am," Lisa replied, taking the shirt distastefully between thumb and forefinger. "I wouldn't be caught dead in this."

"How do you think I feel?" Carole commented. "If you're wearing it, that means I'm Stupid."

Stevie sat back on her heels. "Come on, you guys. You're playing the nasty stepsisters, remember? They're supposed to be mean and obnoxious and generally yucky. You have to look the part, right?"

Lisa didn't answer. Carole leaned over and tried to peer into the bag. "If she's wearing that, what am I wearing?"

"This," Stevie said, pulling out another shirt with a flourish. This one was a Hawaiian shirt with a pattern of surfing dogs on it. The colors were so loud that Carole strongly suspected that whoever had bought it must have been wearing sunglasses at the time.

"No way," she said. "That thing will scare the horses."

"It scares me," Lisa added helpfully. She had slung her T-shirt over the paddock fence and was leaning against the rails next to it.

Stevie glared at her friends. "You've got to wear

them," she said. "Come on. They'll look great with breeches and boots."

"What are you going to be wearing while we're wearing these?" Carole asked. "Not that I'm agreeing to anything," she added hastily.

"I didn't bring my costume today," Stevie said. "But in the scenes where you're wearing these outfits, I'll be wearing my oldest jeans and a white T-shirt with a lot of dirt and smudges on it."

"Oh, you mean the same thing you wear every day," Lisa said.

Stevie rolled her eyes. "Very funny," she said. "For your information, it's all about symbolism. Real film-makers are very big on that, you know."

Carole leaned back on her hands. "Oh, yeah? What exactly do jeans and a T-shirt symbolize?"

"Well, the T-shirt is white, right?" Stevie said. "And you know the good guys always wear white. The beat-up jeans just symbolize how overworked I am—I mean, how overworked Cinderella is. Your shirts will show that the stepsisters are loud and obnoxious and overbearing. Get it?"

Lisa shrugged. "I guess that makes sense, sort of. But what are we supposed to wear in the big ball scene? Hot pink prom gowns?"

"I wish," Stevie said. "Unfortunately I couldn't think of a way to get my hands on any of those. And it would mean you'd have to ride sidesaddle, and that would take more practice." She paused and dug around in the duffel bag again.

"Oh no, I can hardly bear to look," Lisa said with a groan, covering her eyes.

But when she heard Carole's shriek of laughter, Lisa couldn't resist peeking. Stevie was holding up a pair of riding hard hats. But these were no ordinary hats. Stevie had glued rhinestones, feathers, beads, and buttons all over them, so that they sparkled in the afternoon sunlight.

Lisa gasped. "Whose hats are those under all that junk?" she asked.

"They're Max's," Stevie admitted. "I figured he wouldn't miss a couple for a week or so." Max kept a large collection of hard hats in the locker room for the use of Pine Hollow's riders. It had been easy for Stevie to swipe a couple and smuggle them out in her bag.

"Maybe not, but he's sure going to notice them when you put them back," Carole pointed out.

"Don't worry," Stevie said. "I'm going to take this stuff off when we're finished. I used invisible glue. They'll be as good as new when I return them."

Lisa had walked forward to get a better look at the hats. "Wow," she said, with admiration in her voice. "Those are really hideous."

"Thanks," Stevie said with a grin. "See, I was thinking about what you guys could wear to the big dance. Finally I decided the easiest thing would be to have you wear regular show-jumping clothes to show that you're dressed up, and just let the hats symbolize your personalities."

Carole reached out to touch one particularly huge and gaudy fake emerald. "What will you be wearing while we're wearing these?"

"Same thing, sort of," Stevie said. "I'll have a band of flowers around my hat instead of this other stuff. I haven't made that yet, though, since I want the flowers to be fresh when we film."

"I see," Carole said.

"So you'll wear this stuff, right?" Stevie said.

Lisa and Carole exchanged glances. Then, in one voice, they said, "No."

Stevie gaped. "What do you mean, no?" she said. As if it wasn't hard enough being director, scriptwriter, special effects specialist, choreographer, and prop person, now she was having trouble as costume designer as well. "You have to wear these costumes. Otherwise there's no movie."

"Look, Stevie," Lisa said. "We're not sure what's going on, but you're not going to trick us so easily this time. We know you're up to something."

Carole nodded. "We just don't know what it is."

Stevie decided enough was enough. She had to convince her friends, once and for all, that all she was interested in doing was finishing her school assignment. And she had to make them see that she meant it when she said she was through with practical jokes for good.

"I'm like the boy who cried wolf," she muttered under her breath. "Now that I've quit, they won't believe it."

"What was that?" Carole asked.

Stevie dropped the hats back in the bag and stood up. "I said I'm feeling kind of hungry," she said. "How about a trip to TD's?" That was the name of the ice cream parlor at the local shopping center. It was a favorite site for Saddle Club meetings, and that's what Stevie had in mind right now.

"Sounds perfect," Lisa said, and Carole agreed.

TWENTY MINUTES LATER the girls were seated in their favorite booth at TD's. They had placed their orders—Lisa for a hot fudge sundae, Carole for a scoop of butter pecan, and Stevie for marshmallow and pineapple sauce on pistachio—and were sipping their glasses of water while they waited for the waitress to return.

So far the conversation had revolved around Prancer. Now that they had started making a little progress, Lisa and Carole wondered if there was any way Lisa could still compete the following Saturday.

Stevie wasn't taking part in this conversation. She was playing with her spoon and trying to think of a way to convince her friends that she really needed their help, and that she wasn't trying to trick them in any way.

Finally she had an idea. "Hey, you guys," she said. "Why don't we make Prancer's jumping trouble an official Saddle Club project? That way we're sure to figure it out."

Carole looked a little surprised. So far Stevie hadn't seemed very interested in Prancer's problem at all. But maybe she had just realized how serious it was. "That's a great idea, Stevie," she agreed.

Lisa nodded. "If we put our heads together, maybe we'll come up with something brilliant."

"Good." Stevie smiled. "Now, I have another good idea." She paused and took a sip of water.

"What?" Lisa asked expectantly. "Is it something to help Prancer? Or is it a way to get revenge on Veronica for what she did?"

Stevie shook her head. "None of the above," she said. "It's an idea for another great Saddle Club project."

"What is it?" Carole asked.

Stevie tried to think of a dramatic way to explain, but she couldn't. Finally she decided to just come out and say it. "It's my film project," she said. "I really need your help if I want to get a good grade on it."

Carole and Lisa laughed. "We should have known," Carole said. "You're not going to trick us that way, Stevie Lake."

"Trying to get us to think the whole thing is a Saddle Club project," Lisa said, shaking her head and smiling. "How dumb do you think we are?"

"Why won't you believe me?" Stevie cried, dropping her spoon and waving her hands in dismay. "The assignment is for real. I told you I've given up practical jokes, and it's true."

Lisa moved her water glass out of range of Stevie's wildly waving hands. "'The lady doth protest too much, methinks,'" she quoted. When Carole gave her a puzzled look, she added, "Shakespeare. It's from *Hamlet*. It means the more Stevie claims she's given up practical jokes, the less I believe her."

"Oh yeah?" Stevie demanded. "I haven't played one all week, have I?"

"Not that we know of, no," Carole said warily.

Lisa nodded. "But all that proves is that the next one will be a real doozy," she said. "We know you too well, Stevie Lake. You'll never stop joking. Especially since we just helped Phil play such a good one on you."

Carole started laughing again. "Right," she said. "Good old Rex Starr, Hollywood agent. That was great!"

Just then the waitress arrived with their orders. Stevie started eating hers immediately, but she hardly tasted it. Carole and Lisa had already returned to their conversation about Prancer. Stevie's plan had failed. Her friends still didn't believe *Cinderella* should be a real Saddle Club project. But if she didn't convince them, they'd believe it soon enough—when she was banned from Pine Hollow for failing her moving image class.

STEVIE STOOD UP and stretched. Her back was aching and her hands were tired, but she had finally finished gluing multicolored sequins onto every inch of an old Pine Hollow pitchfork. She had managed to sneak it out of the stable that day after her Tuesday riding lesson without Max or Red noticing. She just hoped they didn't notice it was missing until she was finished with it.

"Voilà," she told herself out loud. "The magic pitchfork." The magic pitchfork was the enchanted object that the magical talking lucky horseshoe would conjure up to allow Cinderella to finish her stable chores in time to go to the royal dressage ball. It was an important prop, and Stevie was glad she'd finally finished it.

Stevie left the pitchfork drying on the newspaper she'd laid out on the floor of her room and hurried over to her desk. It was almost bedtime, and she still had a lot to do. Her film was due on Monday—just six days away. And with the Pony Club competition coming up on Saturday, Stevie knew she would be lucky to finish on time, especially since she hadn't shot a single minute of the movie yet.

She sat down at the desk and checked the list she had made. "Magic pitchfork—check," she said, crossing it off the list. She had already finished making several other props that evening, including the sign announcing the royal dressage ball and the cellophane-covered flashlight that would give the lucky horseshoe a magical blue glow.

The next item on the list was to come up with some kind of veil for the wedding scene. Stevie had toyed with the idea of asking Max's wife, Deborah, if she could borrow her veil. But then she had decided that a piece of white netting and a little lace attached to a riding hat would work just as well. The only question was when she was going to have time to make it, especially since she still had half a dozen other things on her list.

Stevie sighed and scratched her chin, where a little bit of glue was drying. She was running out of time. If she wanted this movie to be perfect, she wasn't going to have any time at all to practice for the hunter competition. She hadn't ridden Belle at all for the past week except in rehearsals and today's lessons. And when the rest of the class had been clearing each fence in perfect form—except for Prancer, who was still hesitating before every jump—Stevie had been trying to remind Belle just what jumping was all about. The mare had been too frisky to pay attention to her rider's instructions, and Stevie knew it was probably because she hadn't been exercised enough lately.

All things considered, Stevie wondered if she should even bother taking part in the competition. Not only was there little or no chance she could place in the competition, but she could really use the extra time to work on her movie. Besides, she didn't relish the idea of watching Veronica diAngelo ride away with the blue ribbon.

"Poor me," she whispered, feeling very much like Cinderella herself. There was so much to do, and nobody was willing to help her. She had to do it all herself, even if it meant missing the ball—or, rather, the Pony Club competition.

"Stevie?" Alex poked his head through her open doorway.

Stevie looked up. She was in no mood for her brothers that night. "What do you want?"

But instead of answering, Alex just grinned. "Say cheese," he cried. Then, before Stevie could move, he leaped into the room and snapped a picture.

Startled and partially blinded by the flash, Stevie let out an outraged shriek. "What do you think you're doing?" she yelled.

"Remember how I joined the staff of the school newspaper this term?" Alex said gleefully. "Well, I just snapped the picture that's going on the front page of the next edition!"

"What?" Stevie cried. She jumped up and ran to the mirror over her dresser, blinking her eyes to get rid of the spots the flash had caused. Peering at her reflection, she saw that in addition to the spot of dried glue on her chin, she was sporting a red sequin right in the middle of her forehead and a splash of poster paint on her left cheek. Her hair was a mess, and a pen was stuck behind each ear. Worst of all, she was wearing her oldest pair of pajamas, which just happened to have pictures of baby bunnies all over them.

"Gotcha," Alex said with a wink. He remained in the doorway clutching the camera, poised to run as soon as Stevie came at him.

But she didn't. Instead, she just slumped back down in the desk chair. "Go ahead and print it," she said tonelessly. "I don't care."

"Huh?" Alex looked surprised, then suspicious. He tucked the camera behind his back. "Is this some kind of trick?"

"No," Stevie replied. "I don't expect you to believe me, though. Nobody else does."

"What do you mean?" Alex asked. He still looked suspicious.

"I mean I've given up practical jokes. For good."

Alex laughed. "Yeah, right."

"That's what everyone says," Stevie said with a shrug. She listlessly poked at a stray paper clip. "But I don't care anymore. It's true, and *I* know it, even if nobody else does."

"But why?" Alex asked.

Stevie quickly explained about her teacher's speech and her own thoughts afterward. "So I figured I was better off playing it straight," she said. "I didn't want to get in any more trouble than I already had."

"That doesn't sound like you, Stevie," Alex said.

"Usually trouble is your middle name. And I thought you liked it that way."

"Maybe I used to," Stevie replied. "But maybe I've changed."

Alex took the camera out from behind his back. "You? Change? I doubt it," he said skeptically.

"Believe it or not, I don't care." Stevie started picking the sequin off her face.

"Hmm," Alex said, leaning against the door frame. "Your story really isn't very convincing at all. And that makes me think it just might be true. But I can't help thinking this could be some kind of a trap." He shrugged. "I don't know, Stevie. I want to believe you this time. I really do. But why should I?"

Stevie thought fast. She never would have expected it, but Alex sounded almost ready to believe her. "Well, for starters," she said, "you should believe it because I knew you were going to the movies with your new girlfriend, Susie, on Sunday afternoon, and I didn't even think about going to the same show and throwing popcorn. And I saw Chad practicing his soccer moves right below my window the other day after dinner, and I never for an instant considered filling a few of the balloons I have right here in my desk drawer with water and dropping them on his head.

And I noticed that Michael left his favorite football jersey lying in the living room last night, and I had absolutely no plans to throw it in the washing machine with my red socks so the numbers would come out pink." Stevie paused and looked at her twin. "Should I go on?"

Alex held up his hands. "No, no," he said. "I guess I'm convinced—for the moment, anyway. And if it's true, I have to admit it's too bad. You were good, Lake—really good. It's a shame if you've really turned your back on all that talent. *If* you really have, that is. After all, you can't blame me for still being a little suspicious."

"I guess not," Stevie said glumly. "Goodness knows you're not the only one. Carole and Lisa don't believe me, and neither does Phil."

"Are you surprised?" Alex twirled the camera strap around his finger. "If you ask me, they'd be idiots to believe you, considering your record."

Stevie sighed. "I know. And I guess it doesn't help that I'm trying to convince them to wear weird costumes and act in a wacky movie at the same time I'm trying to get them to believe I've given up practical joking."

"No kidding," Alex agreed. He grinned. "Actually,

when you think about it, that's kind of a practical joke in itself, isn't it?"

Stevie looked up. Her brother had a very wicked look on his face. Stevie recognized the look, because it was one she had seen in the mirror many times. It meant his mind was working in a very interesting way. "What do you mean?" she asked.

"Isn't it obvious?" Alex replied. "They're probably going crazy right now trying to figure out what you're going to do next. They're so sure you're playing a joke on them, when actually there's no joke at all. So they can think about it twenty-four hours a day, but they'll never be able to figure out what you're really up to. Because what you're really up to is . . . nothing. It's brilliant!"

By now, Stevie was grinning right along with her twin. "You know, you may be on to something, Alex," she said. "In fact, you may have just given me a great idea about how to save my movie. . . ."

97

BY THE TIME Carole, Lisa, and Phil arrived at Pine Hollow on Thursday afternoon, Stevie was ready for them. First, she had convinced Carole and Lisa to wait at their school for Phil's mother to pick them up. That would give her a few more minutes, and it would also ensure that they all got to the stable at the same time. If they didn't, her plan wouldn't be nearly as effective.

Luckily the weather had turned rainy again, and Carole and Lisa had eagerly agreed to the ride. Stevie herself hardly noticed the rain as she raced over to Pine Hollow as soon as the final bell rang. She couldn't wait to get there and find out if her plan was all set. It was.

"I don't know, Lisa," Carole said as she climbed out of Mrs. Marsten's car. "She's getting better, and she's doing it at her own pace. I don't know if we should rush her."

They were talking about Prancer again. The mare was jumping almost every time Lisa asked her to now. She *was* getting better, but not fast enough for Saturday's competition. The girls knew they were lucky Prancer hadn't been scared off jumping for good, but they still couldn't help wishing they had more time.

Lisa sighed. "Maybe I should just skip the show," she said. "Or I could try another horse. Max offered to let me ride Delilah if Prancer isn't in shape for Saturday."

"You'll never win a ribbon that way," Phil pointed out. "Switching horses at the last minute will throw you off, won't it?"

Carole nodded. "Phil is right. Prancer is the horse you work with the best. And she's a much better jumper than Delilah."

Phil waved as his mother turned the car around and headed back down the driveway. Then all three of them scurried through the drizzle and into the warm, dry stable.

"Whew!" Lisa said, shaking the water out of her hair. "What a day."

"I hope it doesn't rain on Saturday," Carole said. The three of them went into the student locker room so that Carole and Lisa could change from their school shoes into their riding boots. "The weather has been so unpredictable lately."

Lisa sat down on the bench and pulled off her sneakers. "If it rains, I'm sure Max will just move the competition to the indoor ring," she said, tossing the sneakers into her cubby. "But it would be a little crowded."

"Speaking of the indoor ring," Phil said, "I guess that's where we'll be rehearsing today." He was leaning in the doorway, waiting for the girls.

Carole nodded. "I wonder when we're going to find out what Stevie's really up to," she said.

Lisa laughed. "I don't know," she replied. "But this has been quite a setup, even for her."

"You don't suppose she could possibly be telling the truth about this movie, do you?" Phil asked. "It wouldn't be the first time she's had to redo a project because a teacher didn't appreciate her sense of humor."

"It's possible," Carole said, pulling on her boots and standing up. "But even if the movie is for real, all her talk about giving up practical jokes has got to be setting us up for something."

Phil chuckled. "I guess you're right about that," he said. "Well, come on. If you're ready, let's go tack up."

"Not necessary," said Stevie brightly, coming up behind him. She was holding her prop bag in one hand and the camcorder in the other. "I got here a little early, so I tacked up all your horses for you. They're waiting in the indoor ring. So come on, let's get started."

Stevie's friends exchanged glances as they followed her. Had she heard them talking about her? They hoped not. She had seemed a little edgy lately, and they didn't want to make her angry. But if she had heard anything, she didn't show it. In fact, she was whistling gaily as she walked toward the entrance to the indoor ring.

"Here we are," she said, stepping back to let her friends enter first.

The moment Carole, Lisa, and Phil stepped through the doorway, they heard a man's voice shout, "It's about time! Do you think we have all day? We've got a movie to make here! Now hustle!"

Lisa jumped, startled. Prancer, Starlight, Belle, and Diablo were tied up on one side of the entrance, but she hardly noticed the horses. That was because there was a much stranger sight in the center of the ring. A tall man was striding impatiently back and forth, tap-

101

ping a riding crop on his thigh. There was a director's chair behind him, with a bullhorn sitting on it. The man had a large, carefully waxed mustache, and he was dressed improbably in riding breeches, high boots, a blue silk shirt, and a beret. A bright red scarf was knotted around his neck. Strangest of all, he was wearing sunglasses, even though there was no hint of sunlight coming through the high windows from the gloomy day outside.

"Wha—" Carole began, but the man cut her off.

"Step lively, boys and girls!" he barked, slapping the riding crop on his gloved hand. "Mount up, and hurry up about it. There's a lot to do. We're running through the dressage ball scene first; then we're going to practice the bowing entrance and the wedding parade. Move it, people!"

Carole, Lisa, and Phil automatically started hurrying toward the horses. Carole got there first and swung up into Starlight's saddle. Phil followed suit with Diablo.

Lisa had one foot in the stirrup and was about to swing herself onto Prancer when she paused. What exactly was going on here, anyway?

"Hey, wait a minute," she said. She turned to look at Stevie, who was still standing in the entryway, grinning her head off as she filmed the whole strange scene with the camcorder.

Carole, who was in the process of leaning over to unhook Starlight's lead rope, looked down at Lisa. She frowned. For the first time, she stopped to think. Who was the man shouting at them from the center of the ring?

Phil figured it out at the same time as the two girls. All three of them turned. And all three of them cried out the same name at the same time.

"Stevie!"

Stevie responded by starting to laugh. Soon she was laughing so hard that she could hardly hold the camcorder straight. A second later, the man in the sunglasses started laughing, too.

Lisa took her foot back out of the stirrup. She looked at the man. There was something familiar about him, but she didn't recognize him until he removed the sunglasses—*and* the mustache.

Carole gasped. "It's Mr. French," she exclaimed. Michael French was one of Max's adult riders. He worked for the State Department in nearby Washington, D.C., and boarded his horse, Memphis, at Pine Hollow.

"You caught me," Mr. French said good-naturedly

in his normal voice, a pleasant southern drawl. He tucked his riding crop under his arm and began to untie the scarf from around his neck. "I guess I'd never be mistaken for a real Hollywood director, would I?"

"Don't be so sure," said Carole ruefully. "You had us fooled for a few seconds, anyway."

By this time Stevie had come forward to join her friends. Lisa turned to her.

"So was this what the big joke was all along, Stevie?" she asked.

Stevie shook her head. "Nope," she replied. "The big joke was, there *is* no joke. But since you guys didn't believe me, I thought I'd give you what you wanted. That way, maybe you could forget about practical jokes for a while and I could get my movie made."

Phil looked surprised. "You mean you did all this to get our attention?"

Stevie grinned. "I have to admit, I was inspired by A.J.'s phone call the other day. I decided it was time to go Hollywood myself. Luckily, Mr. French agreed to help me out."

Mr. French came over and dropped his beret, mustache, scarf, and sunglasses into the duffel bag at Stevie's feet. "Glad I could help," he said. "I always thought I should be in the movies. If you need another actor for your film, Stevie, you know where to find me!" He threw Stevie and her friends a mock salute and hurried off.

"So we were right," Carole said after the man had gone. "You never intended to give up practical jokes at all."

"Wrong," Stevie said, fiddling with the buttons on the camcorder. "I meant every word. But desperate times call for desperate measures. I figured I had to break my vow just this once—if only to prove to you that I really meant it. You guys wouldn't listen to me long enough to let me convince you any other way."

Lisa thought about that for a second. She realized Stevie was right. Lisa, Carole, and Phil hadn't really given her a chance to explain before. Lisa and Carole had been too busy worrying about Prancer, and all three of them had been too ready to jump to their own conclusions about Stevie.

"Sorry," Lisa said. "I guess we shouldn't have been so quick to doubt you. Can you forgive us?"

"Well, I don't know," Stevie said, rubbing her chin thoughtfully. "It all depends."

"On what?" Phil asked.

Stevie grinned. "On whether you're all going to buckle down and help me make this movie. I really do need to get a good grade on it, you know. Will you help me?"

"Of course we will," Carole, Lisa, and Phil said in one voice.

And that's exactly what they proceeded to do.

9

"How did it go last night?" Carole asked as soon as Stevie walked into the stable on Friday.

Stevie shrugged. She looked tired. "Not bad," she said. "Not good, but not bad."

"What happened?" Lisa asked, looking up from Prancer's mane. She was in the process of untangling a knot. Carole was helping out by rubbing the mare down with a soft cloth.

"My mom made me stop editing and go to bed around midnight," Stevie said, rubbing her eyes. "That means I didn't get as much done as I should have."

Thanks to Stevie's prank, Carole, Lisa, and Phil had

put in a hard afternoon's work the day before, and Stevie had filmed plenty of footage. Lisa had even come up with a way to end the standoff over Stevie's silly costumes, which she and Carole were still reluctant to wear, practical joke or no practical joke. Stevie had compromised and agreed to let her friends wear their fanciest riding clothes for the early scenes—*if* Lisa could borrow some real ball gowns for the dressage ball scene from the charity resale shop where her mother volunteered. With one brief phone call, it was all settled. Half an hour later, a very confused Mrs. Atwood dropped off three fancy gowns in the girls' sizes. Best of all, Stevie's was a pearly white one with puffy sleeves, which could easily double as a wedding gown in the final scene. After trying on the filmy yellow gown Mrs. Atwood had brought, Carole was even willing to wear Stevie's fancy hard hat as part of her costume. It took all of Stevie's powers of persuasion, but finally Lisa was convinced as well. After all, the stepsisters *were* supposed to be tacky and obnoxious. And that was fine with the actors—within reason.

The matter of riding in a long dress was a little tricky, but Stevie managed to make Max's single sidesaddle work three times as hard by moving it from horse to horse and filming each girl separately, one at a time. It all took a long time and was a lot of work, but Stevie was sure it would be worth it. As head costume designer, she had to admit that the ball gowns would look a lot better on film than the "I'm with Stupid" T-shirt.

Once the matter of the costumes was settled, everything else had gone fairly smoothly. The dressage ball scene was a little trickier with the sidesaddle, but Stevie kept Phil in the foreground most of the time to hide any problems the girls had riding in the unfamiliar position. For the bowing scene Stevie wanted to show both stepsisters entering together. So Lisa, in the sidesaddle, had been in the foreground. Carole had perched precariously in the background in a sidesaddle position on a normal saddle. Luckily both Starlight and Prancer "bowed" perfectly on command at the first try, and the scene had required only one take.

Stevie had filmed most of the other scenes from several different angles, just like a real director. She had hurried straight home after the final scene was on tape and spent almost every minute from then until midnight editing her film. She knew part of her grade would depend on her putting the scenes together in the best way, choosing the best angles and views just like a real filmmaker has to do. She also still had to add music to the sound track and do the opening and closing credits.

"Have you seen Red?" Stevie asked her friends. "I wanted to go thank him again for helping out." Red had stepped in as cameraman for the scenes all four actors were in together, and he had done a fine job.

"He's out on the trail with an adult class right now, I think," Lisa replied. "You can thank him later. Right now, you should get Belle and do some practicing for tomorrow!"

Stevie nodded and yawned. Then she said good-bye to her friends and wandered off toward her horse's stall. The truth was, she had almost forgotten that the competition was the next day. Somehow, her mind wouldn't focus on it. She thought it was because she still wasn't completely satisfied with her film—and it wasn't because there was more editing to be done. There would be plenty of time to finish that on Sunday.

No, the problem was with the movie itself. It had romance. It had excitement. It had the best dressage/ballroom dancing scene ever put to film. All the special effects had gone off without a hitch and were wonderfully convincing on camera. Carole and Lisa had thrown themselves into their roles as the nasty stepsisters, and they were deliciously wacky and wicked. Phil made an incredibly handsome Prince Charming, of course. And Stevie had allowed Lisa to act as hairdresser and makeup artist before her big scenes, so that, she had to admit, she made a pretty spectacular Cinderella. In fact, Phil had been so impressed with Stevie as Cinderella that their big, romantic kissing scene had lasted even longer than Stevie had intended—and the best part was, Carole and Lisa had started hooting and hollering in the middle of it, which meant they had to do it over. And neither Stevie nor Phil had minded that one bit.

So why did Stevie still feel there was something missing?

"Maybe you can help me figure it out," she whispered to Belle. But the horse just snorted in reply.

A few minutes later all three girls were practicing in the outdoor ring. The weather had turned nice again after yesterday's gloominess.

"It's too bad it wasn't like this yesterday," Lisa called to Stevie, who was trotting Belle over a row of cavalletti, concentrating on controlling the length of her strides. "You could have done your filming outside."

"That's okay," Stevie said. "The lights in the indoor

ring were bright enough. It looks almost like daylight on film." She was glad that Belle seemed to remember her training pretty well, even though Stevie hadn't had much time to work with her.

Stevie and Carole both stopped what they were doing and turned to watch as Lisa took Prancer through the small jump course she'd set up in the center of the ring. Prancer jumped every fence without knocking down a rail, but Carole and Stevie could see that Lisa wasn't having an easy time getting her to do it. Prancer still hesitated before every jump, and Lisa had to urge her forward insistently with all her aids. That meant her scores in the hunter competition would be low, since the whole performance had a rough, choppy look and Lisa's aids were much more noticeable than they should be for hunter jumping.

For the first time, Stevie started to put her mind to Lisa's problems. Lisa had helped her out yesterday, and now Stevie wanted to return the favor if she could. "What do you think is holding her back?" Stevie asked as Lisa rode over to join her friends near the gate.

Lisa shrugged. She was breathing hard after the strenuous ride. "I don't know," she said when she caught her breath. She patted Prancer on the neck. "I had hoped she'd gain some confidence after she saw she could do it a few times without trouble. But she still seems nervous."

"Try it again," Stevie suggested. "We'll watch her carefully and see if we can get any hints."

Lisa nodded and turned Prancer back toward the first fence. Now that the entire Saddle Club was concentrating on the problem, maybe—just maybe—they could figure out what to do.

They took the course again. And again, Prancer jumped cleanly but awkwardly, ruining her form with her jerky pauses before each obstacle.

Lisa was shaking her head as she rejoined her friends. "Exactly the same," she said grimly. "Any ideas?"

Carole had to admit that she didn't have a single one.

"I have an idea," Stevie said. Lisa and Carole turned to her hopefully. "My idea is that we should take a break and go on a trail ride."

Her friends looked surprised. "But the competition is tomorrow," Carole pointed out. "Don't you think we should do all the practicing we can today?"

"There's such a thing as overpreparing," Stevie said.

Her friends thought that was a little strange, since

as far as they knew Stevie and Belle had hardly prepared for this competition at all. But they had to agree that a trail ride sounded like a wonderful idea.

The three girls rode out of the stable yard and headed across the fields toward their favorite wooded trail. They kept their horses at a walk, not wanting to tire them too much the day before the competition. At first they didn't talk. They just rode, enjoying the nice weather and each other's company.

When they entered the woods, Lisa turned to glance at Stevie, who was just behind her. "The usual spot?" she asked.

Stevie nodded. Carole did, too.

A few minutes later, The Saddle Club had reached their favorite spot—a shady area overlooking the creek that had given their hometown of Willow Creek, Virginia, its name. They dismounted and headed down to sit by the tumbling stream, leaving their horses to rest and munch on the new spring grass that was just poking its way up in the clearing.

Lisa settled down on a large, mossy boulder and sighed. "This is nice," she said.

"It sure is," Stevie agreed. She perched on a smaller rock nearby and rested her arms on her knees.

Carole took a seat on the grassy bank of the creek.

"It's been a while since we've been on a trail ride, hasn't it?"

"It's been too long," Lisa agreed. "I guess that's because we've spent so much time trying to fix Prancer's jumping problem"

"And I've been busy with my film," Stevie added.

"That reminds me," Carole said. "I wanted to apologize again about that, Stevie. I was thinking about it last night, and I realized we really weren't fair about the whole thing."

Lisa nodded. "That goes double for me," she said. "We should have believed you when you said you'd given up practical jokes." She paused. "Although in a weird way, I'm kind of sorry you turned out to be serious about that. Even though your pranks sometimes got to be too much, I have to admit I'm going to miss them."

Carole nodded in agreement. She had been thinking the exact same thing. Somehow Stevie just wouldn't seem quite as, well, *Stevian* when she wasn't playing practical jokes all the time.

Lisa went on. "Anyway, we should have realized you really needed serious help with your film. Especially when you asked us to make it a Saddle Club project."

"Right," Carole said. "After all, that's one of the

most important things about being a member of The Saddle Club—asking for help and being sure you'll get it."

"Don't worry about it," Stevie said with a wave of her hand. "It's all water over the bridge now. Or is it under the bridge? I can never remember. Anyway, the important thing is that you guys came through in the end."

"I'm glad we wised up in time," Carole said, rolling over on her stomach to examine a small blue flower that was sprouting nearby.

"Stevie made us wise up, remember?" Lisa corrected her. She smiled. "That was pretty clever, Stevie, getting Mr. French to play movie director! It really got our attention."

Stevie grinned and shifted to a more comfortable position on the rock. "That was the point. And I think he had fun doing it, too."

"Anyway," Carole said, rolling onto her back once again, "the point is that it shouldn't have been necessary."

Lisa nodded. "We should have trusted you in the first place, Stevie."

"That's okay," Stevie began. "Like I said, it's all—"

Carole suddenly sat bolt upright. "That's it," she said.

Stevie and Lisa stared at her. "What's what?" Lisa asked.

"That's the answer to your problems with Prancer," Carole said. "When you just said we should have trusted Stevie, I realized that trust is the key to your jumping problems, too."

"What do you mean?" Stevie asked.

But Lisa had already figured it out. "You mean Prancer has to learn to trust me completely again before she'll jump for me?" she said. She flicked an ant off her leg and shrugged. "I guess that's probably true. But what can I do about it? After all, I didn't have anything to do with that alarm going off in the first place. How can I convince her I can keep it from happening again?"

"I don't know," Carole admitted. "I just know that if you can get her to trust you as much as she did before, she'll be able to jump just as confidently as she did before."

"Easier said than done," Lisa murmured. She knew Carole was trying to be helpful, but she didn't see what good it did to know that Prancer didn't trust her fully. Even if Lisa hadn't put it in quite those words before, it had been obvious from the beginning that that was at least part of the problem.

Stevie frowned. "I can't believe Veronica managed

to cause so much trouble with one little prank," she said. "It makes me gladder than ever that I decided to give up . . ." Her voice trailed off, and she looked thoughtful.

"What is it, Stevie?" Carole asked. Stevie had a very odd look on her face. It was the look she got whenever she came up with one of her wild schemes.

Carole and Lisa traded hopeful glances. Did this mean what they thought it meant? Was their friend Stevie ready to take up her crown again—the crown of Master of Practical Jokes?

Suddenly Stevie grinned. "I think I just figured out what's missing from my film," she said mysteriously. "And I also think I've got the perfect way to get back at Veronica for messing up your jumping, Lisa. I've just got to work out a few important details. . . ."

Carole and Lisa laughed and leaned forward to exchange high fives with their friend. The old Stevie was back!

"WHAT DID RED SAY?" Lisa asked Stevie. It was Saturday, and the Pony Club hunter competition was scheduled to start in thirty minutes.

Stevie grinned and gave a thumbs-up sign. "He said we can go ahead," she replied. "For a second I thought he was going to say no, but then he decided to play along—or rather, play dumb. I think he's still mad at Veronica for that personal alarm thing, too."

Lisa grinned back. Stevie's latest scheme was up and running, and the good news was that Veronica di-Angelo was going to pay—but big. The bad news was that Lisa still wasn't sure what to do about Prancer.

After the trail ride the day before, she had taken the mare through the jump course several more times. Prancer had been as hesitant as ever.

Finally, Lisa had given up and returned the mare to her stall, hoping that a miracle would happen overnight. But she knew better than that. When it came to training horses, there were no miracles, just hard work. Still, it seemed a shame to accept a low score in today's competition when Prancer had come this far. It would be like letting Veronica win—in more ways than one. And no Stevie Lake revenge plot, no matter how clever, would be able to change that.

Carole was in Starlight's stall when Veronica arrived twenty minutes later. The competitors were due in the ring in less than ten minutes, and the gelding was tacked up and ready to go. He seemed to be in good spirits, and Carole had high hopes for his performance in the competition. He was ready, and so was she. When she heard the familiar shriek of anger, she grinned. Giving Starlight a quick pat, she let herself out of the stall and hurried down the aisle toward Danny's stall.

When she arrived, Stevie and Lisa were already there. Lisa was holding the Lakes' camcorder in one hand, and both she and Stevie were trying hard not to laugh. Veronica was standing in the aisle, holding

Danny's lead line and practically hopping up and down with fury.

Danny gazed down at his owner, unperturbed and not seeming to realize or care how ridiculous he looked. His mane and tail were intertwined with gaudy multicolored ribbons. His legs were carefully wrapped with neon orange bandages. His sides were striped with an intricate pattern of painted black lines, making him look a little like a zebra. And someone had painted a bright-yellow smiley face right in the middle of his forehead, just below the brow band of his bridle.

Carole grinned when she saw that. It was a real Stevie Lake touch. "What did she use to paint that on him?" she whispered to Lisa.

"Nontoxic poster paint," she whispered back. "The stripes, too."

Carole was impressed with Stevie's cleverness. She had known the basics of the plan. But her contribution had been to tack up Belle and Prancer, as well as Starlight, so that her friends could get Danny ready before Veronica arrived. So she hadn't seen the results until this minute. Now that she saw them, she knew the plan was brilliant. There was no chance Veronica could get Danny looking normal again in the next ten minutes. And there was even less of a chance that the snobby girl would ride him looking like some kind of weird circus horse.

"He looks, um, wonderful," Carole said with a giggle. She glanced at Veronica. "You must be so proud."

Veronica whirled angrily to face her. "You shut up, Carole Hanson," she screeched. "I know why you three jerks did this. You all want Danny and me out of the show because you can't stand the competition. You knew we'd win."

Out of the corner of her eye, Stevie saw that Lisa had raised the camcorder and was taping the scene. Luckily Veronica hadn't noticed. "Get real, Veronica," Stevie said, tossing her head. "There's no way you could beat The Saddle Club. Not on your best day and our worst."

"Ha!" Veronica put her hands on her hips and glared daggers at Stevie. "What a joke! Danny's the best horse in this entire stable, and I'm a better rider than all three of you put together. You're just jealous, that's all. You're jealous of me, and my horse, and—and—"

"And your horse's wardrobe?" Stevie supplied helpfully.

Veronica just sputtered for a moment. Her face turned redder than ever. Finally she found her voice again. "I hate you, Stevie Lake!" she shrieked, her hands clenched into fists. "I hate you! I wish I had my personal alarm with me today! I'd set it off again, and this time I'd make sure I did it while you were riding so you'd fall off in front of everybody! Then we'd see what you had to say!"

Lisa's eyes widened. This was an unexpected bonus. Not only was Veronica confessing to setting off her alarm on purpose, but she was doing it on tape! She kept the camera rolling, not wanting to miss a thing.

Suddenly Veronica noticed what Lisa was doing. "What's that?" she snapped. "A camera? Turn that off! Who gave you permission to film me?"

"She just wants some candid shots of Danny looking his best," Carole piped in. "Maybe the local TV station will want to show them on the news tonight."

Veronica snarled at Carole, then turned back to Lisa. "Turn that off right now, I say!" she yelled. "Turn it off, or I'll turn it off for you!" When Lisa didn't respond, Veronica tried to carry out her threat. She lunged at Lisa with an outraged shriek, her newly manicured fingernails splayed like weapons.

Lisa jumped back out of range, a little worried. She had never seen Veronica so angry. Luckily, at that moment Red O'Malley stepped out from around the corner. Moving calmly and smoothly, he stepped over to Veronica and grabbed her firmly by both arms.

"That's enough of that, Veronica," he said quietly.

"What are you doing?" Veronica screamed. By now her long black hair had come loose from its neat braid. One strand had fallen into her face and gotten stuck in her freshly applied lipstick. "Take your hands off me!"

"Not until you calm down," Red said firmly.

Veronica struggled for a few seconds, then seemed to realize that Red was much stronger than she was. Finally she held still. "All right," she said icily. "I'm calm. Now let me go."

Red did so. "Are you all right, Lisa?" he asked.

"I'm fine," Lisa replied. She switched off the camera and glanced at Stevie. Stevie winked, looking pleased as punch.

Red glanced at Danny, who had been watching the entire scene disinterestedly. "You're lucky you didn't spook your horse," he said.

Veronica tossed her head. "Danny's a pro," she said. Her voice was returning to its normal haughty tone. "And now that you're here, you can help me get this ridiculous getup off him so we can be ready in time for the competition. Max will just have to let us go near the end."

Red shook his head. "I don't think so, Veronica," he said. "Once Max hears that you set that alarm off on purpose, you're not going to be in any shows here for a long time."

Stevie grinned. This was turning out even better than she had planned.

"What do you mean?" Veronica asked with a frown. "My personal alarm went off by accident. I told Max that when it happened."

"But you just told these young ladies something different," Red said. "I was in the next aisle, and I clearly heard you say you set the alarm off the first time and wished you could do it again."

Veronica shrugged and started to tuck her hair back in place. "You must have misunderstood," she said, smiling calmly. "I'm sure I said no such thing."

"I'm sure you did," Lisa said. She held up the camera. "And what's more, I can prove it."

Veronica's calm smile changed to an expression of rage. Once again, she launched herself at Lisa. But Red caught her again.

"Come on, Veronica," he said grimly. "Let's go have a little talk with Max, shall we?" As he dragged her away, he glanced back at The Saddle Club. "You three wouldn't mind looking after Danny, would you?"

"Of course not," Stevie called after him. "We're always glad to help out!"

* * *

125

LISA GULPED DOWN a knot of nervousness as she trotted Prancer around the front paddock to warm her up. There were only two more riders to go, and then it would be their turn.

She turned and watched as Polly Giacomin rode into the ring. Polly's horse, a brown gelding named Romeo, jumped a little when the audience began to applaud, but he calmed down quickly.

"At least you're used to the roar of the crowd, right, girl?" Lisa told Prancer quietly, giving her a pat. In her days as a racehorse, Prancer had had to deal with much larger crowds than this. There were dozens of people watching the hunter competition, including the members of the new Pony Club and their adult chaperones, the young riders from Pine Hollow who had already ridden or hadn't gone yet, and a number of parents and adult riders who had come to watch. At one end of the ring sat the three judges, Max, Red, and Mrs. Reg. Max's wife, Deborah, sat nearby in front of a table of gaily colored ribbons that would be awarded at the end of the show. Phil was standing next to her, chatting with Mr. French.

Lisa watched as Polly and Romeo went through the course. They began at a smooth and even pace and approached the first fence perfectly. Romeo nodded his head a little after he had cleared it, as if congratu-

126

lating himself, and Lisa smiled. The pair went over the next three fences just as easily, but at the next one they ran into some trouble. Romeo didn't lift his hind feet enough as he went over, and his hoof clipped the top rail, bringing it down with a clatter. The noise seemed to unnerve him, and he brought a rail down on the next fence as well. The audience groaned in sympathy. After that, Polly managed to steady him, and they finished the course without another major fault. She looked disappointed as she tipped her hat to the judges, and Lisa didn't blame her.

"We all want to do well today, don't we?" she murmured to Prancer as Polly rode out of the ring and the next rider rode in. "At least, I know I want to do well. And I hope you do, too." She sighed as she said it. Despite their best efforts, The Saddle Club hadn't been able to come up with a solution to Prancer's jumping problem.

Lisa dismounted and led Prancer out of the paddock. They were next. She walked toward the gate, wishing that Stevie and Carole were there to give her some final words of wisdom. But Stevie had performed just before Polly and was inside with Belle, and Carole was over near the paddock helping one of the other riders untangle a stirrup. Lisa was on her own.

"I don't know how I can convince you to trust me,"

she whispered to Prancer as they waited their turn. "You'll only do that when you're ready. I just wish you were ready today!" She was dreading their round. If the audience had groaned at Polly and Romeo, how would they respond to Prancer when she practically came to a stop before every fence?

It was time to mount. Lisa swung up into the saddle and gathered up the reins. "This is it, girl," she told Prancer. "It's all in your hands now. Or rather, your hooves." She giggled a little despite her nervousness.

Then she stopped. She thought about what she had just said. It really was all up to Prancer now. If she decided to trust her rider, they could have a good round. If not, it would be a disaster. But Lisa had just realized something. How could she expect Prancer to trust her when she didn't trust Prancer?

"That's it," Lisa whispered as the crowd applauded politely for the rider who was just finishing. Ever since the accident, she had been expecting Prancer to have trouble, and she had. But what if she expected her to do well? Would it work? She didn't know. But she couldn't think of anything else to try.

"Next rider: Lisa Atwood on Prancer," announced Mrs. Reg over the small loudspeaker. The crowd applauded politely as Lisa rode into the ring.

"Okay, Prancer," she said, just loud enough for her horse to hear. "I'm leaving it all up to you now." She clucked to the mare and sent her once around the ring at a smooth trot. Then she steadied her with the reins and aimed her toward the first fence.

*Relax*, Lisa thought to Prancer as they got closer. Or was she thinking it to herself? Soon they were just four strides away, then three . . . Was Prancer starting to slow down, or was it Lisa's imagination? She signaled firmly for the horse to continue. Two strides . . .

This time there could be no mistaking it. Prancer was trying to stop. Lisa signaled once again, then sat perfectly still, letting the mare make up her own mind. If she didn't want to jump the fence, Lisa wasn't going to make her this time. But if she did want to . . .

She did. At the last stride, Prancer hesitated for a moment, and Lisa heard a few gasps from the crowd. But then the mare went ahead and jumped the fence—without any urging from Lisa. At the next fence she didn't hesitate at all. She jumped the rest of the course clear.

Lisa was grinning when she finished. She stopped to salute the judges and saw that Max was grinning, too. "Good job, Lisa," he mouthed at her. And that made her grin even harder.

\* \* \*

"FOURTH PLACE!" LISA squealed, hugging Carole again. Carole hugged her back.

Stevie clapped her on the back. "Great job, Lisa," she exclaimed. "I can't believe you did it. She looked great out there!" Both Stevie and Carole had finished what they were doing just in time to watch their friend ride. And they had both been there to cheer when Deborah had handed Lisa her fourth-place ribbon. Lisa had cheered just as loudly for her friends when Carole and Starlight had been awarded first place and Stevie and Belle had won second. A rider named Adam Levine had come in third.

"Thanks," Lisa said. She glanced into the stall behind her, where Prancer was munching on some well-deserved carrots. "But I didn't really do anything. It was all Prancer."

"This calls for a celebration," Carole declared. "TD's, anyone?"

Lisa nodded. "Count me in," she said. She would never have believed coming in fourth could feel so good. Usually she wasn't completely happy unless she was first. But this time, coming in fourth felt just as good as winning. And she knew that the next time, she and Prancer would give Carole and Stevie a run for their money.

Stevie shook her head. "Count me out," she said sadly. "I can't go. I have to get back home and work on my film if it's going to be ready for Monday."

"Poor little Cinderella," Carole teased. "You mean you can't even take a break for a quick sundae?"

"No. Sorry," Stevie said, and she looked it. She knew her grade was on the line, and now that she had the extra footage she needed to make her film perfect, she wanted to get right to work. "You two go ahead. And have an extra scoop for me."

"Okay," Lisa said. "Just as long as it doesn't have to be raspberry ripple with caramel sauce!"

THE FRIDAY MORNING after the Pony Club competition, Stevie filed into the Fenton Hall auditorium for morning assembly along with the rest of the students. But unlike the rest of the students, Stevie had a huge grin on her face. That was because her movie was going to be shown to the whole school.

After the headmistress had finished her usual string of announcements and sat down, Ms. Vogel stood up and faced the audience. "It's time for another film," she said with a smile, holding up a hand for quiet as the students began to applaud. The moving image teacher had already shown several other students' films in previous weeks, and her audience had been very appreciative. After all, the more time they spent watching films, the less time they had to spend listening to boring lectures on school fund-raisers.

Stevie held her breath as Ms. Vogel loaded her tape into the video projector. She glanced around until she spotted Veronica, who was busy filing her nails a few rows ahead. Stevie grinned harder than ever. She had the funniest feeling that Veronica would be particularly interested in her film.

The lights went down, and the movie started. The opening credits rolled. Then the picture faded up to reveal the familiar setting of Pine Hollow's stable row. Stevie was there, dressed as Cinderella, mopping her brow and mucking out a very dirty stall.

"Oh, dear me, what shall I do?" Stevie-as-Cinderella exclaimed on the tape. "My terrible, mean stepsisters have left me to clean out the stable all by myself. Oh, poor me—poor Cinderella. Will my pathetic life ever get better?"

But the best part of all came a few seconds later. Stevie had edited the film to insert some of the footage Lisa had shot of Veronica's tantrum, but she had recorded over Veronica's voice with the new dialogue she had written for Veronica's part, the wicked stepmother. Stevie had convinced Alex to read the part, and he had done a wonderful job, making his voice high and witchlike, complete with evil cackles. So all the audience saw was Veronica's face twisted up into a terrible grimace, while the voiceover cackled, "Hurry up now, my pretty. There's lots more chores for you to do. And when that's done, you'll help my lovely daughters get ready for the royal dressage ball, or there'll be no bread and water for you tonight!"

The audience roared with laughter. It was a fairly small school, and everyone knew Veronica diAngelo, at least by reputation. Seeing her in such an atypical role was a big surprise to everyone.

But the most surprised person of all was Veronica herself. She glanced up from her nail file to see what everyone was laughing about. It took a second for her to recognize herself, and when she did her face twisted up into a snarl that very much resembled the one she wore on-screen. She whirled around and gave Stevie a withering glare. Then she hunched down in her seat and tried to make herself as small as possible. But it didn't help. Her classmates laughed helplessly, turning one by one to grin at her or point her out to their friends.

Veronica made several other appearances throughout the movie. Since Stevie only had a few minutes of footage to work with, she had had to use some of it more than once. Somehow, that made it even funnier.

134

Best of all was the moment when Red—or rather, the prince's loyal manservant—had stepped forward to save Cinderella from the wicked stepmother's fingernails of death when she found out her stepdaughter was marrying the prince. Veronica's "line"—"I'll scratch your eyes out, my pretty!"—sounded completely convincing when paired with Veronica's wild-eyed run straight at the camera. By the time the movie ended, Veronica's face was redder than the glossy crimson nail polish she was wearing.

After the assembly, Stevie tried to make her escape, but she was mobbed by students wanting to congratulate her on the film. That made it easy for Veronica to find her.

"I guess you think you're pretty clever now, don't you, Stevie?" she hissed, brushing past several girls who were asking Stevie where she'd gotten the ball gowns. "But I'm not going to stand for this. I'm going to tell your teacher you filmed me without permission. Then we'll see how much she likes your little movie."

Stevie gulped. She hadn't really thought about that. If Ms. Vogel found out what she'd done, she would be in big trouble—just as she had been when she'd filmed Alex without his permission. Before she had time to think of a plan, she saw Ms. Vogel approaching, a proud smile on her face.

"Congratulations, Stevie," she called out. "It seems you're a hit!"

Veronica turned, an unpleasant smile on her face. "Hello, Ms. Vogel," she purred. "I'm glad you're here. I need to talk to you about something. Something important."

Ms. Vogel held up one hand, still smiling. "Don't say a word," she told Veronica. "I think I can guess what you want to talk about, and I just want to say that I've been thinking the exact same thing."

"Huh?" Veronica looked confused.

Stevie was confused, too. What was Ms. Vogel talking about?

The teacher put one hand on Veronica's shoulder. "You wanted to talk about the drama club play, right?" she went on. "I'm sure you've heard by now that we're going to start casting Shakespeare's *Antony and Cleopatra* next week. And after your terrific performance in Stevie's movie, Veronica, I think you're a shoo-in for the part of Cleopatra. You really nailed the role of the wicked stepmother—what a convincing performance! I think you show a lot of talent and some real potential as an actress. Congratulations—and I hope I'll see you at tryouts next week."

Veronica's jaw dropped. So did Stevie's. She couldn't believe it. Ms. Vogel was really convinced

136

that Veronica had been acting! But that wouldn't do her any good if Veronica ratted on her.

Veronica didn't. She just smiled at the teacher. "Thank you so much, Ms. Vogel," she said sweetly. "I'll definitely be at tryouts. I'd love to play Cleopatra."

The teacher congratulated both girls again, then walked away. As soon as she was gone, Veronica's smile changed back to a frown. "Don't think this means you're off the hook, Stevie," Veronica said. "I'm still not happy about what you did."

Stevie knew that just because Veronica hadn't told on her now, it didn't mean she wouldn't change her mind later. But she was beginning to see a way to make sure that didn't happen. She shrugged and sighed dramatically. "Well," she said slowly, "maybe you're right. Maybe I should go catch Ms. Vogel and confess. I'll tell her you weren't acting at all, that I filmed you totally without permission—"

"No!" Veronica interrupted. "Um, I mean, that's not necessary. What's done is done." She smiled tightly. "I suppose I don't really see any need to tell her the truth about this. But you have to promise to keep quiet, too. Ms. Vogel may be clueless, but she's right about one thing. I *am* a great actress. And if she thinks that little prank of yours proves it, who am I to argue? After all, it could get me the chance to play Cleopatra."

Stevie shrugged again, feigning uncertainty. "Well, if you really think that's a good idea . . ."

"Of course I do," Veronica snapped. "So just keep your mouth shut, Stevie Lake, and you won't get hurt." She turned and wandered away, looking thoughtful and muttering something about Cleopatra and Elizabeth Taylor and glamorous costumes.

Stevie watched her go, the grin on her face bigger than ever.

"IS THE POPCORN READY?" Stevie asked, hurrying into her family's living room. She held up a video cassette. "Because here's the main feature."

She pushed the tape into the VCR and joined Carole and Lisa on the couch. Carole had just finished making a big bowl of popcorn, which was sitting on the coffee table in front of them, along with tall, cool glasses of soda. It was Friday evening, and The Saddle Club was having a sleepover at Stevie's house.

"I can't wait to see this masterpiece," Lisa said with a grin, taking a handful of popcorn. Carole and Lisa had been so busy all week that this was the first chance they'd had to see Stevie's movie. They knew that Ms. Vogel had shown *Cinderella* at the school assembly that morning, which made them more eager than ever to see the film.

Stevie clicked the VCR on with the remote control. Then she leaned back to watch. No matter how many times she saw her movie, she never got tired of it.

Carole and Lisa squealed when they saw themselves on tape. They looked grumpy and mean and obnoxious; in other words, exactly the way the wicked stepsisters were supposed to look. And they laughed until they cried when they saw Veronica as the wicked stepmother. Stevie's idea to make Veronica an unwitting star in her film had sounded funny when she'd first proposed it. But now that they were seeing the result, Carole and Lisa had to agree that it was hysterical.

By the time the screening was over, Carole and Lisa were laughing so hard that they had completely given up on the popcorn. As the final credits finished, Stevie hit the rewind button on the remote control. Then she turned to her friends expectantly. "Well?"

Carole and Lisa caught their breath, looked at each other, grinned, and broke into loud, enthusiastic applause.

"I have to admit it, Stevie. You're a cinematic genius!" Lisa said.

Stevie stood up and took a bow. "Thank you.

Thank you," she said. "I promise never to forget the little people who helped me when I'm the toast of Hollywood." She sat down again and smiled. "The best part is, my teacher agreed with you," she said. "She said this film was truly clever. And she realized how much work I put into it. After all, it's not easy being director, scriptwriter, special effects specialist, choreographer, prop person, costume designer, and film editor all rolled into one. Not to mention star, of course. It's more than even Cinderella herself ever had to do. So Ms. Vogel is forgiving my last film completely. I got an A-plus on the project."

"That's great!" Lisa exclaimed. "So your riding career is safe again."

"Until the next big project is due, at least," Carole added with a grin, reaching for her soda.

"No way," Stevie said, leaning back on the couch and propping her feet up on the coffee table. "I'm not letting myself get in that situation again. From now on I'm going to be more careful."

Lisa raised an eyebrow. "Does this mean you're sticking with your no-practical-jokes vow?"

"Well, maybe not completely," Stevie admitted. "They're too much fun to give up for good. And they can come in pretty handy sometimes, like when it's time to give Veronica a taste of her own medicine. But

I *am* going to cut back a little. This whole thing has taught me that there's a time and a place for everything, including practical jokes. I just have to think more before I act, and decide before each prank if the rewards are worth the risks."

"Don't tell me all those lectures from your parents and teachers have finally sunk in," Carole teased.

Stevie shrugged. "Nah. What really got me was the way you guys didn't believe me about my movie."

"We said we were sorry about that," Lisa reminded her.

"I know, and I said I forgave you," Stevie said. "But I was thinking about it, and I realized that I hadn't given you much reason to trust me about stuff like that."

The girls munched their popcorn silently for a moment, thinking about what Stevie had said.

"Well, I guess we've all learned something about trust lately," Lisa said at last. "After all, it was only when I learned to trust Prancer that she got over her jumping problem."

"You know, I'd almost forgotten about that already," Carole said. "Prancer did so well in lessons this week."

Lisa nodded. "She has been great, hasn't she?" she said. "She's an awfully smart horse. And brave, too.

Once she realized I was leaving everything up to her, she just went for it. She sensed how much I was trusting her and decided to go ahead and trust me back."

"You're awfully smart, too," Stevie said. "I'm not sure I would have figured that out." The tape had finished rewinding, and she hopped up to eject it.

"Stevie's right," Carole said, chewing thoughtfully on a piece of popcorn. "You did great, Lisa. It just goes to show how far you've come since the first time Veronica spooked your horse."

"Thanks," Lisa said. She smiled. "And I almost met my goal for the show this time. Prancer's pace was pretty steady after that first jump, right?"

"Right," Carole said. "I guess I did okay on my goal, too. Starlight only jumped a little when everyone applauded him this time." She turned to Stevie. "Hey, that reminds me. You never did tell us what your goal for the show was."

Stevie shrugged. "Isn't it obvious?" she said. "My goal for the show was to survive it. And it was looking iffy for a while there." Her friends laughed, and Stevie smiled. "Actually, I did have one other goal," she added. "And that was to place better than Veronica if I possibly could."

"Hmm," Carole said. "I'm not sure Max would approve of that goal. But I guess you did it!" She picked up her glass and saluted Stevie with it.

Stevie picked up her glass, too. "I sure did," she said. "Thanks to The Saddle Club!" She clinked her glass against Carole's. Lisa quickly picked up her glass, too, and clinked it with both of her friends.

"You did even better than that," Carole said, setting her glass back on the table. "You not only managed to keep Veronica out of the show, you managed to get her kicked out of Horse Wise again, too."

"Not really," Lisa pointed out. "Veronica did that herself."

"True," Stevie agreed. She grinned at the memory. Max had been so angry when Red had told him about Veronica's accidental confession that he had ordered her off the property immediately. He had also revoked her Pony Club membership indefinitely.

"By the way, what did Veronica think when she saw her movie debut at the assembly today?" Lisa asked.

Carole gasped. "Oh, I forgot all about that! She must have been livid!"

"Oh, she was," Stevie assured them, crossing her arms behind her head and leaning back against the couch with a self-satisfied grin. "Luckily, Ms. Vogel is convinced Veronica is just right for the role of Cleopatra." She quickly told her friends about what had happened after that morning's screening. "So I'm not sure whether to expect horrible revenge from Veronica or not. But if she wants to try anything, I'll be ready."

Lisa shook her head with a rueful smile. "Uh-oh. Here we go again."

"Don't worry," Stevie said. "If Veronica does try anything, I'll just have to carefully balance the rewards of getting her back against the risks, and then consider if and how I'm going to respond. It might not even be worth it, you know."

"That's very mature of you, Stevie," Carole commented.

Stevie shrugged. "It's the new me," she said. "Calm, cool, collected, and mature." She stood up. "This popcorn is good, but I'm still hungry," she said. "How about some cookies? My mom just made them today. Oatmeal raisin."

"Great!" Carole said, and Lisa nodded eagerly. Mrs. Lake's oatmeal raisin cookies were famous throughout the neighborhood.

Stevie hurried out to the kitchen and returned a moment later with a plate piled high with delicious-looking cookies. Carole and Lisa each grabbed one and bit into it immediately.

Stevie picked up a cookie, too, but she didn't take a

bite. Instead, she watched her friends, a mischievous grin on her face.

Carole chewed for a second. Then a very strange expression crossed her face. She started chewing more frantically, reaching for her soda glass at the same time. She glanced at Lisa, who had a similar horrified expression on her face. Both girls quickly took huge gulps of soda, washing down their mouthfuls of cookie.

Then, in one breath, they gasped, "Stevie!"

Stevie grinned. "Oops," she said. "My mistake. I must have given you my own secret-recipe jalapeño eggplant cookies instead."

Lisa groaned. "I guess this means the real Stevie is back."

Carole nodded. "And you know what that means." She grabbed a sofa pillow. Lisa did the same.

"Ready?" Lisa said.

"Ready," Carole said. "Aim, and fire at will. Pillow fight!" With that, they began pummeling Stevie with the soft cushions.

Stevie grinned as she grabbed another pillow and tried to defend herself from her best friends. The rewards of this particular practical joke had definitely been worth the risks. Definitely. It felt good to be back.

# ABOUT THE AUTHOR

BONNIE BRYANT is the author of many books for young readers, including novelizations of movie hits such as *Teenage Mutant Ninja Turtles* and *Honey, I Blew Up the Kid*, written under her married name, B. B. Hiller.

Ms. Bryant began writing The Saddle Club in 1986. Although she had done some riding before that, she intensified her studies then and found herself learning right along with her characters Stevie, Carole, and Lisa. She claims that they are all much better riders than she is.

Ms. Bryant was born and raised in New York City. She still lives there, in Greenwich Village, with her two sons.

Don't miss Bonnie Bryant's next exciting
Saddle Club adventure . . .

# SILVER STIRRUPS
## The Saddle Club #65

Carole Hanson is used to being the best junior rider at Pine Hollow Stables. She's taken it for granted in a quiet, nice way. She doesn't need to brag about something that she's good at, that she loves with all her heart, and that she plans to make her life's work. Then a new rider starts taking lessons at the stable. She's younger than Carole, and she's a better rider. Carole is jealous, and this new feeling is ruining the place she loves best. Maybe being number one means more to her than she thought!

Carole soon realizes that the new student excels in the saddle, but on the ground she's got a lot to work out. With dread, Carole also realizes that she is the best person to help this motherless young girl with her problems. But can she forge a friendship with someone she envies? Carole is fighting a battle with jealousy—and it looks like the green-eyed monster is winning!